THE BADLANDS SALOON

A NOVEL

written & illustrated
by
JONATHAN TWINGLEY

Scribner
New York   London   Toronto   Sydney

SCRIBNER
A Division of Simon & Schuster, Inc.
1230 Avenue of the Americas
New York, NY 10020

First Scribner hardcover edition July 2009

For information about special discounts for bulk purchases,
please contact Simon & Schuster Special Sales:
1-866-506-1949 or business@simonandschuster.com

The Simon & Schuster Speakers Bureau can bring authors to your live event.
For more information or to book an event, contact the Simon & Schuster
Speakers Bureau at 1-866-248-3049 or visit our website at www.simonspeakers.com.

Text set in New Baskerville

Manufactured in the United States of America

1   3   5   7   9   10   8   6   4   2

Library of Congress Control Number: 2008048924

ISBN: 978-1-4165-8706-4

For Helen

"Heh-yup!"
 —WILLIE BECK

THE BADLANDS SALOON

Rooftop Cocktail Parties

My grandma had an uncle who lived to be nearly a hundred years old. His name was Abraham Running and he never had a regular job, he never married and he didn't have any kids. Abraham Running had no conventional role in the world, and he certainly wouldn't have fared very well in the world we live in now. Uncle Abe was a strange kind of character—a Bible-beater who never went to church, a hand-rolling cigarette smoker, a hot-dog-eater and he only ever took a bath when he absolutely had to. He made a slim living as a painter, but not for galleries or museums. Abraham painted barns and houses and bedrooms in western North Dakota a hundred years ago, before the Interstate Highway was born. He lived with a black Labrador in a little lean-to out on the open prairie after his family disowned him, but he wasn't unhappy. I visited him for the first time one summer when I was in college and he had some great stories to tell me and we laughed a lot. He was ninety-six years old when I met him.

One time when he was young and looking for work, he told me, a woman had hired him to paint blue polka dots on her unborn baby's bedroom ceiling. Abraham showed up at this woman's house that evening with his worn-out paint brushes and a bucket of baby-blue house paint. She invited him into the house and showed him the bare little bedroom where she wanted the polka dots painted on the ceiling. She gave Abraham a ladder and left the room. Abraham Running had never gone to school, but he was a clever man. He climbed the ladder up to the ceiling of the bedroom and used the paint can lid as a stencil to trace out the polka-dot circles on the ceiling with a lead pencil. He did this while the woman was out of the room, and he did it artfully, tracing the polka dots onto the ceiling to reflect the Little Dipper and Polaris—the North Star—somewhere out there above them in that prairie celestial sky.

As Abraham dipped one of his worn-out brushes into his can of baby-blue house paint he was distracted—the woman who'd hired him was on her hands and knees on the bedroom floor, frantically spreading out copies of the *McKenzie County Farmer,* the local newspaper.

"What're you doin'?" Abraham Running asked her from up there on the ladder, a half-lathered brush in his hand. "I can't read and paint at the same time!"

I felt a little bit like that a few summers ago. I was healthy and young, studying how to be an artist at a famous New York City art school in Lower Manhattan, trying to read the writing on the wall. It was an expensive art school and I'd come to New York City with a firm understanding of who I was: Six foot four, lanky, homegrown and a little bit handsome, I suppose, in an innocent sort of way, curious, too, eyes wide open. But how do you study to be an *Artist?* That turned out to be the only thing I wanted to know from the teachers there and it was costing me a lot of money to ask the question. After a year in New York City I'd been to about a thousand rooftop cocktail parties, and at each one about nine out of ten people, when asked *"What do you do?"* usually answered: "*Oh, I'm an Arteest.*" Video Arteests, Installation Arteests, Performance Arteests, Protester Arteests, Cardboard Arteests, a whole Crayola boxful of flashy people who could describe themselves a lot better than I could. I wasn't so sure. Things were still in the oven for me. New York City wasn't just a fork in the road, it was a portal to a universe that was going to take some figuring out and I was always suspicious of those kids who already had job descriptions. I was figuring out that I'd been an *Arteest* all my life, and also that that word—*Arteest*—wasn't taught in grammar schools in North Dakota. We spelled the word differently where I grew up.

I'd sent out a single graduate school application six months earlier. I was about to graduate from the little liberal arts college I'd been attending in western Minnesota, just across the Red River from Fargo, North Dakota. I had researched graduate schools a bit, but applied to only one in the end, a rather prestigious art school in New York City. I put the application in the mail just for the hell of it, on some level, because I had to do *something*. A bachelor's degree in *Art* doesn't carry a lot of water in this world, and there was always that practical little part of my brain that said: *"Listen, sonny-boy, if you get a master's degree you can teach someday, and you'll probably have to, because it doesn't make any sense making a living painting pictures. Use your head."*

But I had never laid awake at night in North Dakota dreaming of leaving, like some kids did. I'd always been pretty much content wherever I was. I was just like that, I guess, content to spend my days and nights drawing and painting, way out of my head in whatever was happening on the canvas at the time. I didn't need to go anywhere to really travel. Art is like that.

As it turned out, though, my application to the art school in New York City was accepted and it was time for me to pack a bag. I'd been living with my parents that summer in Bismarck, which is the capital of North Dakota, pretty much smack-dab in the middle of the state, right there on the Missouri River. For money I'd been traveling around the Upper Midwest—South Dakota, Minnesota, Montana— drawing five-dollar caricatures of people at outdoor art festivals, exaggerating their noses and ears and eyes all out of proportion for a quick laugh. It wasn't *High Art,* what I was doing, but it paid my tuition each fall and I assumed the money would spend the same way in New York as it had in Minnesota.

And whenever I imagined the campus of the art school I saw a sprawling-lawn campus like the university I'd been studying at in Minnesota, with trees and fountains and gardens. I arranged for a car to pick me up at the airport—just me, a suitcase and a bagful of brushes and pens and sketchbooks. If you've ever taken a car into Manhattan from LaGuardia Airport you know that monumental feeling and the raging butterflies you get crossing the bridge over the East River, the buildings-upon-buildings rising up in front of you like in an animated film, but nothing Mickey Mouse about it, a concrete Grand Canyon that not even Walt Disney himself could've ever dreamed up.

I'd given the driver the address of the dormitory I'd signed up for on Twenty-third Street and Lexington Avenue—a formerly grand hotel called the Livermore. He dropped me off, I paid him and he left. And there I was: No sprawling-lawn campus in sight, no gardens or fountains, just the screams of taxicabs roaring down Lexington Avenue and the people-herds, the beggars and the beauties. I was in shock. In hindsight, I should have tried better to more realistically imagine where I was going, but I didn't and the reality was incredibly exciting/terrifying/out-of-body, all at the same time. Because I'd never really even thought about a world beyond my mom and dad and little brother back there in Bismarck, or the lazy little college town in Minnesota. *How could anything even really exist outside of that world I grew up in?* Sure, I'd seen the cities of the world in late-night cable TV movies, but those were all just fiction to me, just somebody else's fantasy. I had all sorts of fantasies, but my whole real world had been North Dakota, and I'd been more or less happy there in that world, content.

I checked into my tiny little room at the former old hotel and saw my first New York City cockroach. That first week I only left the building for slices of pizza across the street at the Pakistani/Mexican deli/pizzeria. The rest of the time I spent looking out my dormitory window with a sketchbook, just drawing the traffic and the people with a pencil, trying to put everything in perspective, trying to make this new world *real.*

The graduate program I enrolled in was a good one. There were sixteen or seventeen other students with me in the program, a diverse group of people—several Koreans, a woman from Italy, a kid from Santa Fe who was really into Zen Buddhism, who carried himself solemnly and made pictures of flowers and streams and rocks. There were a couple of middle-aged students, too, taking a break from their real worlds to blow off some steam. There was a girl from California and a comic book artist from Long Island. And me. I was the token Midwesterner, it turned out, but that wasn't especially unique because nobody's unique in New York City.

It was a two-year program, after which I'd be *Oliver Clay, Master of Fine Art,* or at least that's how the paper would read. That first year involved the usual things—projects and critiques, lots of walking around exploring the city, drawing and painting in the studio till the early-morning hours. It was a spectacular world and a spectacular time in my life. The second month I was in New York City, Allen Ginsberg gave a reading at St. Mark's Church down in the Village—right there where he lived—where he and Jack and Bill Burroughs had bent all those minds. It was a rainy night and the wind was whipping around Twenty-third Street and I was walking along there down Second Avenue, happy as the clams. New York City felt like a dream to me. It wasn't Bismarck or Minnesota or wherever I'd ever been before, but someplace altogether new. I was far from home and feeling adventurous, off course and there. There there there.

My cheap little umbrella broke along the way so I threw it into a beat-up old New York City garbage can and got to the church early and wet. Allen Ginsberg was there mingling around, shaking hands and kissing the young boys on the lips. I'd never seen that before, but I knew Ginsberg's poetry well. I'd read *Howl* on the roof of the art department building back in Minnesota at sunset and it was a revelation—forceful/free energy that couldn't be tied down by any poetical norms or traditions. It was like a rifle shot reading that poem.

I sat right up in the front row that night at St. Mark's Church, ten feet away from Allen Ginsberg as he read his poems and sang righteous hymns like *Ballad of the Skeletons*. People were whooping and hollering and it was really something to be there. Midway through the evening he was telling a story—setting up a poem—and a lone voice up in the balcony of the church hollered out—kind of a long, loud slur: *"Thhhaaaattt'ss not how it haaaappened, Allen."* It was Gregory Corso, standing up there in the balcony in a haze of blue smoke, leaning against the railing and everybody in the audience down below laughed. Ginsberg looked up at Corso there in the balcony of the church and asked: "Well, how *did* it go, Greg?" The whole thing was a hoot.

The evening raged on and on like that and the rain had stopped by the time the reading was over and I walked back to my little rented room on Lexington Avenue with wings on my heels.

Later that first year I got a call from a classmate of mine saying that Allen Ginsberg had died. She was friends with friends of Ginsberg's and she knew that I liked his energy. She told me that there was going to be a private memorial service for him at a Buddhist temple there in Manhattan the following morning, gave me the address and said to get there early. I was exhausted at the time—I'd been painting all day and half the night—but it seemed like one of those things that a guy shouldn't miss if he can help it, so I walked across town early the next morning, over to West Twenty-second Street to a nondescript building and took the elevator up to the seventh floor. I took off my shoes and entered that little urban temple and knelt down on loafy pillows. There was incense burning and pictures of Allen Ginsberg and flowers on a little altar at the front of the room and eventually the celebrities started to arrive, and then the monks started their moaning and cymbal-clinking, smoke and smoke and smoke. The ritual was intricate and lasted for hours and hours and nobody said a word—at least not in the English language. The whole thing was a long ways from the Sunday-morning Lutheran church services I was used to back in North Dakota. I felt like a spy behind enemy lines, except there weren't any enemies there, just strangers who felt like friends, and poetry.

I went back to my dreary little jailhouse dormitory room on Lexington Avenue that afternoon and made drawings from memory of everyone who'd been there that morning at the Twenty-second Street/seventh-floor Buddhist temple, all the stars and musicians and the lesser celebrities that'd come to pay their respects. I put those drawings into a manila envelope and brought them uptown to *Rolling Stone* magazine on Sixth Avenue—the Avenue of the Americas—because it all seemed like a perfect journalistic piece for them, a guerrilla paparazzi batch of drawings that they wouldn't be able to get anywhere else. I was sure they'd be thrilled to have those drawings.

But I never heard from the editors at that magazine.

It was an exciting year, that first one in New York City, but I hadn't left the Midwest because of any great unrest. I was torn between the two places in a lot of ways. Minnesota, in the fall, when the leaves on the trees were exploding with hot colors on quiet streets, or the Missouri River on the Fourth of July, Bismarck and the State Capitol building—the tallest building in North Dakota—a thousand miles of windblown country roads in every direction, where the cows are your only audience. And New York City with its smells and neighborhoods, pizza delivery boys on bikes, suicidal bicycle messengers and all-night everything; Broadway and Coney Island, Rockefeller Plaza, Fifth Avenue, the Empire State Building and King Kong. New York City was an explosion like a star that might burn itself out someday, but not tomorrow and not anytime soon. Both places made perfect sense to me and I loved both places for different reasons. When you grow up in wide-open, prairie spaces, dreaming becomes a big part of reality. And New York City *itself* was a dream, a real-time movie set where my life—at least for a little while—felt newborn-baby new.

Leaving Home, Going Home

It was the end of my first year at the art school in New York City and I needed a summer away from the hustle and bustle. Art school wasn't all that it had been cracked up to be and graduate school, especially, turns into a great escape for a lot of people—two or four or more years avoiding any sort of real commitments. But that wasn't my case, though, because I was committed to all sorts of things in my mind. I guess I just needed three months away from New York City's laser focus to make things blurry for a while. My life at that point was like a drawing in its early stages and I needed to take a minute and squint my eyes so I could see things more clearly.

So I called Tank Wilson and put my few things in a storage room at the school. Tank Wilson was my friend. I'd known Tank since my Bismarck days. He ran a little bike shop in Marysville, North Dakota, a tiny tourist town on the North Dakota/Montana border. After I'd moved to New York City, Tank had told me that if I ever needed a summer job, he had one waiting for me in Marysville. He'd been working there seasonally for a number of years by then, renting out bikes and leading groups of tourists on rides along lonely cow paths through the Badlands. I knew enough about the Badlands to do that, and could fix flat tires, too, if I had to. I wasn't a whiz when it came to bicycle mechanics, but I knew enough to get by. Tank said he'd put me up in a trailer his uncle owned next to the campground just outside of town if I coughed up the money for the plane ticket. The trailer was called Wigwam. All of the trailers in the little trailer park there had names—Sakakawea, Buffalo Alice, Curly and Custer. It was expensive as hell living in New York City so I decided to take

Tank Wilson up on his offer and head out west for the summer, save some money, clarify my vision and rest my eyes.

Manhattan isn't a very big place. It's just an island. But when you spend any substantial amount of time there, down in the shadows of that concrete world, it feels *bigger* than the world, everything represented there on that sliver of land at least a little bit. The buildings in New York City block out the sun sometimes. I suppose anyplace can feel like that—like the center of the universe—but taking off on a Northwest Airlines flight out of LaGuardia Airport—passing over the city in just a second or two and then heading out over the never-ending hills and plains and mountains of America—it's just as easy to see that even a place like New York City is as finite as everything else.

11

Marysville

North Dakota is a land of extremes. In the wintertime it can get to be a hundred degrees below zero, if you count the windchill factor, and in the summer it gets well *over* a hundred degrees a lot of the time. Marysville in the summertime had a high-desert feel to it—tumbleweeds in the ditches, the wind kicking up some of the oldest dust in the world—and under the rocks the rattlesnakes, waiting for the sun to go down to crawl out onto the asphalt roads and warm themselves in the absolute silence.

Marysville is in western North Dakota, in the middle of the Bad-lands. It's set in a flat, low-lying stretch of dirt surrounded by rocky ramps rising all around, like a crude, prehistoric bowl, the road run-ning from the Interstate Highway down into the town like a blacktop ladle. The Badlands are all that's left of what was once a gigantic inland ocean, full of prehistoric sharks and fish. Marysville was all octopus and seaweed a million years ago, and there are still seashells in the dirt there, the farmers and ranchers will tell you, subtle reminders of a transition from one kind of place to another. Change is the only constant, I suppose, and it shouldn't be any different in the Badlands, and in Marysville. Long after the dinosaurs, the town was a favorite vacation spot for a president of the United States who liked to hunt, and it was home to a rich Frenchman who gave the town its name.

There was an oil boom in the 1970s when the land had been rediscovered as a sort of big natural oil tank, millions of years of bones and autumn leaves laid out beneath the rock and the sage and the sun. The town was a gateway to the underbelly of the earth.

It was like California in the 1800s—rugged men dedicating their lives to dreams of bank accounts buried deep in the ground. Men left their families to find a big future in the hills of the Badlands.

Years later, when the oil pumps slowed down, Marysville made the next evolutionary step in the life of small towns: It turned toward tourism. A state-of-the-art outdoor amphitheater was built outside of town where a musical extravaganza was performed every night all summer long. It was a patriotic show with an aw-shucks, down-home feeling to it, celebrating all the things that the place had been in the past.

In town there was the Old West Shooting Gallery and bumper cars, everything done up in an Old Western style. The sidewalk that ran past the Badlands Saloon and the old-timey pizza parlor was a wooden boardwalk like the ones in John Wayne movies. The town had become a strange version of itself, the old and the new functioning in some sort of syncopation, a generic vision of what towns once looked like when there were cowboys and Indians and wagon wheels and campfires. But there was an authenticity to it all, too. Marysville had been around for so long that it embodied several pasts at the same time, each one elbowing out some room for itself among the newer versions of the *Old Town*.

There was a coffee shop in Marysville, but none of the permanent residents ever considered it necessary because they all had coffeemakers at home in their kitchens on their countertops. Coffee brewed at home was cheaper. The coffee shop was for the tourists who passed through town each summer and shot up the shooting gallery and smashed into each other in the bumper cars. The coffee at the coffee shop was made with well water, and when I was a kid growing up in Bismarck I had a friend who lived in the country outside of town and his house was supplied with well water, too. I always thought that the water at his house tasted like blood, all rich and earthy and metal-tasting. When I asked my mom about it she said something about it being the iron in the water, but I thought it tasted like blood, not like iron. In Marysville, the way the coffee tasted at the coffee shop, that was the *Old* fighting for a place within the *New*.

There were a hundred or so people in Marysville who were more-or-less permanent residents, families whose families had owned land

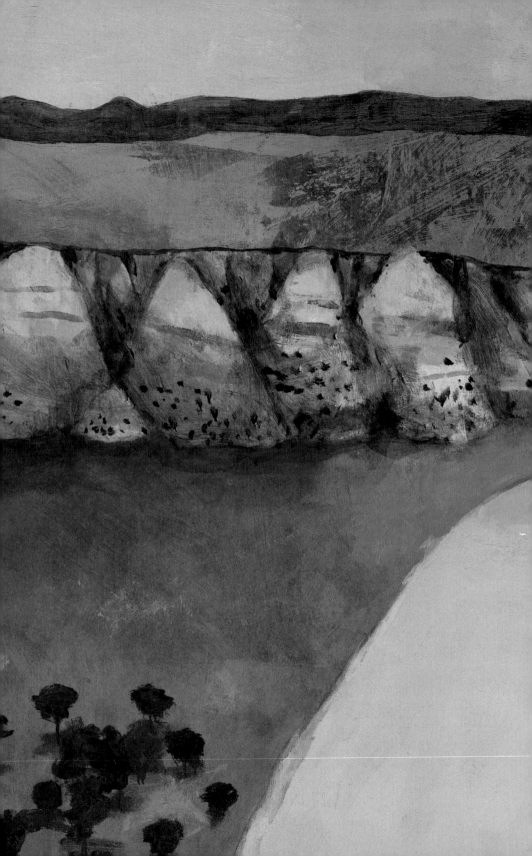

and ranched or farmed there for generations—with varying degrees of success—and they stuck around, adapting to the changes the town had endured. Other locals ran the shops or rented them out to out-of-towners seeking their own gold. The city's mayor, Donald Grinhauser, took tickets up at the amphitheater every evening during the summer. He also owned show horses and had a radio program each afternoon on the local Marysville AM station. Everybody in Marysville—even the mayor—had an odd job or two.

But there was a core group of these permanent residents in and around Marysville that didn't do much of anything, a group disconnected entrepreneurially from any aspect of the Tourist Town, who were never connected with the goings-on of the Boom Town—Willie Beck, Kate, Lacy, Larry, Mildred, Jimmy Threepence and more—all so conspicuous that they went mostly unnoticed, a sort of popular anonymity that was nothing new.

That summer, as I rolled into town on the shuttle bus from Dickinson, I saw a chain gang working on a railroad track that ran along a stretch of the road leading into Marysville. The prisoners were all tied together by chains at their ankles and they looked like a single organic thing there next to the road, a prison-striped dragon in a Chinese New Year's parade, slinging their sledgehammers in rhythm, wedding the spikes to the ties. The Burlington Northern Railroad Company ran right through and past Marysville but it didn't offer passenger service, it only transported things, not people—just coal and corn—and I watched the prisoners swinging their hammers from the window of the bus, watched the two men with rifles and sunglasses watching the prisoners in turn, all of us hotter than hell. We all had all the time in the world. We did.

But I was free.

Chains & Whistles

The shuttle bus dropped me off on Main Street there in Marysville, 21
in front of Tank Wilson's bike shop. The place was called Chains &
Whistles, a funny name for a bike shop, I thought, but Tank Wilson
was a funny guy.

"OLLIE!!" he yelled when he saw me standing out in front of the
shop with my bags. "You made it, man!!!" I thought about how I had
felt nine months earlier, standing on Lexington Avenue in midtown
Manhattan with my bags, fresh from Bismarck—that wild, new feeling of adventure—and how similar and different it felt standing
there on Main Street in Marysville, that feeling of being a stranger in
your own hometown.

Tank walked out with a wrench in his hand and gave me a big
bear hug. "Welcome to our little Wild West Fishbowl, dude!" Tank
always called the place a "Wild West Fishbowl." I suppose in a little
seasonal town like that you did sort of feel like you were swimming
around on the inside of a glass cage, watching all the tourists come
and go, living a straightforward, day-to-day life.

The front of the bike shop was a massive, sliding garage door, flak-
ing white paint and half-rotting boards. The place had been a livery
stable or a metal shop or something else at one point, a hell of an
old building there on Main Street in Marysville. Inside it was like an
airplane hangar with rows and rows of bicycles—some for sale, some
just to rent—a counter with a cash register on it and behind the
counter a workshop area with a couple of bike stands and all of the
assorted tools. There was a boombox on the workbench and out
the backdoor of the shop was Wallingford Creek, the little stream of

water that ran clear through town. Everything about Marysville seemed *little*, coming from New York City, but it all seemed *big*, too, the way a place does when you're in the middle of it.

"How was your flight, man?" Tank asked me.

"Good," I said. "It's good to be back, you know? Everything smells fresh."

"Yeah, give it some time," Tank said. "It'll start smellin' old pretty quick." Tank had a way of grinning at you out of the corner of his eye.

Tank Wilson's wardrobe was halfway in-between junior high and Beat Poetry—baggy khaki trousers rolled up to mid-shin, black T-shirt with a white line drawing of the devil on it, trucker-style baseball cap, lamb-chop sideburns halfway down his cheeks. His wallet was attached to his black belt with a beefy metal chain like a Lower East Side hoodlum. He wore a grease-stained apron around the shop, drank heavy black coffee all day, whiskey and beer all night long, smoked cigarettes out behind the shop next to Wallingford Creek when business was slow. And things were very often slow at the shop there in Marysville because most of the people who passed through town in the summertime were old—blue hair and cheap jewelry in big Winnebagos—or they were motorcycle tourists on big Harley Davidsons, leather-tanned men in shades and windblown girls with tight jeans and tattoos. Not the kinds of people who rented pedal-bikes.

"How's business been?" I asked Tank.

"Pretty shitty and slow," he said. "Just how I like it." Tank was fixing a flat tire. "But the Foundation pays most of the expenses around here, anyway. They like all the shops downtown to look busy in the summertime for the tourists." The Foundation was a public trust set up by the State Tourism Council.

"I love the Foundation," Tank said.

Tank Wilson was an artist with bicycles. All the while he talked his hands fixed the flat tire fluidly, like a puppeteer working the strings. He hardly had to look at what he was doing because Tank's whole life was bicycles. Bicycles and hell-raising. Tank Wilson was always looking for the edge of the line, and when he found it he'd cross it real quick for a second and then bump back to some sort of safety. Working for himself in a bike shop in a little Tourist Town each summer was about all he could handle.

"How's the city, dude?" he asked me. Tank's manner was casual, pretty much the same way as he dressed.

"It's going good," I said. "New York's a long ways from home, but it's going good."

"Raising any hell?" Tank asked me, with that smile-look of his.

"Just drawing and painting," I told him.

Because Tank was a wild spirit, I had a hunch he wouldn't be there in North Dakota for very long. He was in and out of Marysville every other weekend as it was, chasing down some expensive adventure on cheap flights out of Dickinson to Seattle or Denver or San Francisco or Phoenix, his heart always on the move like some hearts are, no anchors, just temporary harbors here and there. Tank was older than me—old enough to be a big-brother figure, I suppose—and he was sharp, too, always had the perfect comeback for wisecrackers. He was recklessly handsome in that James Dean sort of a way, the kind of guy that drove good girls crazy. And everybody envies that bad-boy quality in a young man—men and women alike—because it's something that we're all afraid of, especially when we notice a little bit of it in ourselves. But it's so alive that you just want to get closer to it.

"Must be time for a smoke," Tank said. We walked through the door at the back of the shop. "You much of a smoker?" he asked me.

"Sure," I said, "I'll have one or two every now and then." I wasn't much of a smoker, really, but it just seemed like the thing to do when you went off to college, hanging out in hazy coffee shops playing chess. Tank handed me a cigarette and lit a match. I cupped my hands around the flame and then he lit his own.

"Yeah, man," he said with a big old exhale. "This place is funny."

"How many summers have you been working out here, anyway?" I asked him, toying around with my cigarette. "How long has it been?"

"It's been a few, dude," he said, blowing blue smoke. It was half-shadows out there behind the bike shop. The creek slurped along at our feet. "It's a fun gig, though," he went on. "There's no real pressure, you know? The tourists are a pain in the ass, but that's part of the price for living free out here all summer long." There was a part of Tank Wilson that you could never fully figure out, some part of his personality that you knew he wasn't letting you see. Maybe that was part of his charisma. He flipped his fag into the stream and

watched it drift away for a second. He watched it almost thought-fully. He turned to me, blinked and clapped his hands. "You need a bike, man!"

We headed back into the shop. There was a rack of rental bikes along the west side of that cool, dark room. "You're tall!" he said, looking at me and laughing. He pulled a bike with a twenty-one-inch frame down off the rack at the side of the shop. "See how this one fits," he said.

"A single-speed, huh?" I said, examining the bike. "Looks great to me." It was a bright orange two-wheeler, nearly new without any derailleurs or cogs for gears. Just a couple of brakes. It was a simple way to set up a bike—little or no maintenance required—and there was something almost primal about it that I liked. I'd been a rider for years, but not much since I'd moved to New York City. It was good to feel that simple machinery again. "It's perfect," I told him, straddling the bike.

"Well, all right," Tank Wilson said. "Let's get you out to the trailer. I'll close up early. It's slow as hell around here anyway."

Wigwam

Tank slid the giant front door of the shop closed and padlocked it. I had my book bag with pens and pencils and ink and sketchbooks— all the essentials—and Tank had my suitcase. He had a bike with a sort of fifth-wheel mini-trailer attached to the back of it, for hauling kegs of beer, Tank told me later. He strapped my suitcase to it and we headed out.

Riding a bike again after having not ridden one for a while was a beautiful feeling—like some sort of freedom, silent steady motion, connected to the ground under us because I could feel it, connected to that perfectly blue sky overhead because I could see it, rolling along without a sound. It was five o'clock there in Marysville and everything was crystal clear, the air and the view. I felt like I'd been deeply exhaling ever since I landed back in North Dakota.

We rode the few blocks through town, down to the main road that passed through Marysville off of the Interstate. We pedaled the shoulder of the road a mile or so out of town and turned right onto the gravel road that ran past the town's swimming pool. Beyond the swimming pool was the campground, and just past the campground was the trailer park. Tank's uncle's trailer, Wigwam, was in the middle of the park. It was a simple structure—weathered aluminum on the outside with a rickety little wooden staircase leading to the front door. We parked our bikes out front and Tank untied my suitcase.

"Should we lock 'em up?" I asked Tank, pointing at our bikes.

"Are you crazy?" he said. "This is cow country, man." Tank had a way of saying offhanded things that didn't make any sense on paper

but made perfect sense when he said them. "Who the hell's gonna steal our bikes, the horseflies?" He unlocked the door and led me in. "Welcome home, sucker."

The place was comfortably furnished, but nothing spectacular. It was just about right, I figured, and a huge step up from my room at the Livermore back in New York City. There was a couch along the left-hand side of the living room as you entered—the kind my grandma had back in Bismarck—and a matching love seat on the opposite wall. The kitchen had dishes and a little five-and-dime set of table and chairs from the 1950s. There was even a coffee grinder on the counter.

"There's a coffee shop in town, right?" I asked Tank, pointing to all the mugs and the coffee grinder.

"Yeah," he said, "but I'm partial to a home brew." Tank had been living in the trailer just before I'd gotten to town, when he and his girlfriend were on the outs. Down the narrow hallway toward the back of the trailer there was a small bathroom on the left, and beyond that a bedroom with a nice queen-sized bed, a couple of closets and a little vanity counter where Tank had arranged a bunch of framed photographs—him riding some impossible trail in the Badlands, his mom and his dad, and Lacy, his girlfriend at the time, a radiant Indian girl. I thought she was beautiful and I told Tank as much. "You can have her," he said. He laughed a little and turned back down the hall. I looked at the picture again and thought it was funny that Tank had laughed.

I was overwhelmed by Marysville, on some level, my change of place. The town felt familiar in a general sort of way because North Dakota was home for me—ground zero—and though the towns in North Dakota each have their own specific flavors and feelings, there is a wonderful sameness to them all, too, and not in a generic, limiting sort of way, but in more of a tribal sense: When you're from a place like North Dakota, you're a lifetime member of the tribe.

I walked back out into the main living room area. "Must be time for a smoke," Tank said, offering me a cigarette from his hard-pack.

"Thanks," I said.

There was a little inexpensive turntable on the counter by the love seat. Tank thumbed through a few of his uncle's records and put on a Bob Dylan album. It wasn't Tank's usual choice—Tank Wilson was more Punk Rock than anything else—but maybe his uncle's collection limited him a bit. The needle was dull and skipped ahead on the vinyl: "... *Let me forget about today until tomorrow.*"

That seemed like a sensible line to me.

The Badlands Saloon

I made myself at home that first week there at Wigwam and at the bike shop, too, cleaning up the bikes and just generally keeping things in order. I tried to solicit the passing tourists sometimes, but they didn't show much interest in the bike-rental business. And after work each afternoon I would familiarize myself with the surrounding hills, riding along those lonely old cow paths, over washed-out tabletops of sand, on gravel roads sometimes but mostly off-road, paths carved out of waste-high prairie grass. We'd been warned about the rattlesnakes by the park rangers, but I tried not to think about that too much when I was out there all alone.

It was my first end-of-the-day Saturday in Marysville at the bike shop—a characteristically beautiful day there in the Badlands—and I was glad to be there with my friend in that wide-open, carefree country. I locked down the shop, saddled up my mountain bike and just coasted around Marysville's eight or ten side streets in the setting sun, past a few rows of plain little houses where the park rangers and postal clerks and people like that lived—the full-timers—past the Old Hotel where the actors working up at the musical each summer lived. The streets were quiet most of the time, but it was Saturday night and things were busier than usual on Main Street. It was summertime in Marysville and the Badlands Saloon was one of two watering holes in town where the seasonal employees and the locals bought each other beers. The Badlands Saloon was right next door to Chains & Whistles. I parked my bike below one of the front windows of the bar and went in.

It was an old, flat-fronted building with a roof that sloped down as you went out back toward Wallingford Creek. Inside it was pretty much standard fare: An elegant mahogany bar ran along the right side of the room as you walked in, three quarters of the way to the back, a standard back-bar with all the old familiar bottles in front of a hazy mirror, the same smoky reflector that'd served as a looking glass for thousands of men on thousands of Saturday nights. Off the end of the bar there was a pool table, and behind the table—at the rear of the room—the wall came up too close to the table for a full-sized pool cue, so at some point somebody hacksawed a full-sized cue in half—like you'd do with a shotgun—so you could take a shot from that side of the felt if you had to.

Along the left wall of the room as you came in were three or four booths covered with a cracked red vinyl. The wallpaper throughout the bar was a continuous printed pattern of little cartoon men with shotguns and little cartoon Labradors hunting pheasants. There was a table in front of the window opposite the bar. The light fixtures hanging from the walls and ceiling were wobbly and there were the usual neon beer signs all over the walls of the bar.

And of course there was music from a jukebox, because late-night bars without music are just a bunch of drunk people trying to talk above each other. The tunes helped to stitch it all together. The songbox at the Badlands Saloon was loaded with the usual suspects: Hank Williams Jr. and his dad, Johnny Cash, Willie Nelson, a Bob Dylan album or two. And like most little out-of-the-way bars, the jukebox at the Badlands Saloon had a couple of gems on there, too, like *T. B. Sheets*, that crazy, little-known Van Morrison album. And that song—"T. B. Sheets"—got to be my theme song that summer: *"And the sunlight shinin' through the crack in the windowpane/Numbs my brain, oh Lord . . ."* I'd ask Kate to turn up the volume when that song came on, late at night, swimming in beers and whiskey.

Kate was the bartender and general manager of the Badlands Saloon. She was firmly middle-aged with long, straight, feathered black hair, frozen in a 1970s style. She always wore blue jeans and a black leather Harley Davidson vest, and she treated me like a friend the minute I met her.

"Hey there," she said when I walked into the bar that first night. "What can I get you?" She asked me if I was just passing through and I told her no, that I was working with Tank Wilson for the summer at

the bike shop next door. "Ahhh," she said, "this one's on me." I couldn't tell if that first free drink at the Badlands Saloon was out of sympathy for me or fondness for Tank. Probably a little bit of both. Tank was a wild child, just as likely to break your arm as shake your hand. "Draw a card," Kate asked me after she poured my beer, handing me a plastic bucketful of folded tickets. "Maybe you'll get another free drink." The bucket was loaded with tickets that read *"Two for One"* or *"Fifty Cents"* or *"FREE DRINK!"* It was a Saturday-night ritual at the Badlands Saloon to draw a ticket and drink for cheap or for free so I did, every Saturday night all summer long.

Ultimately, the Badlands Saloon was a perfect hideout. The light was never very bright, even in the afternoons, and the bar seemed to have its own atmosphere, something tangible and thick, the stale smell of cigarette smoke and draft beer. The seats in the few booths had high backs, kind of like caves when you sat at the tables there. It felt almost like you were a primitive man, drinking beer there and building the world's first fire, perfect for someone like Al Capone—who Willie Beck claimed was a regular at the Badlands Saloon when he was younger—or perfect for someone like me, needing a little time to set my course.

The Badlands Saloon was a capsule of the past, present and future, all rolled into one like Einstein's beam of light. Some of the pictures on the wall behind the bar were black-and-white shots of the old settlers and the greasy oil-rushers. There were Polaroids, too, of babies and graduations—Kate at her Senior Prom. But there was an inherent future to the Badlands Saloon, too. The bar was more or less an outcropping of the ancient hills around Marysville by the time I got there and it seemed impossible to consider any sort of future at all in Marysville without the Badlands Saloon, there on Main Street like a lighthouse calling all the sailors home. The Badlands Saloon seemed as real and immutable to me that first Saturday night as anything I'd ever known. It was like the beating heart of Marysville itself—a bank of records, a church, a salon, a group home for everyday foot soldiers. The Badlands Saloon was all of these things and it was a rock, the kind of thing that never really goes away.

Willie Beck

That same Saturday night I met Willie Beck. I heard him before I saw him, actually, something like the sound of schizophrenic thunder—a spitting/walloping cacophony of slurred screams and spittle. I was shooting a game of pool with a guy named Larry, nursing a round of beers and listening to the jukebox. Larry was a carpenter in Marysville, he helped build the sets up at the amphitheater each summer for the musical show. He was a permanent resident, born and raised in Marysville, and he was absolutely content in his life, always smiling, always happy to tell a joke. He wore coveralls and work boots. It was twilight time and the bar was getting smoky. "Your shot."

As I aimed there was an enormous burst of coughs and hacks back at the bar. I turned to look and there he was: A short, frumpy, sweaty little man with horn-rimmed glasses, whacking and hacking, holding on to the edge of the bar for leverage. When he was finished he hollered up toward the ceiling, "OHMARY!!" There were only a few people in the place and the jukebox was playing softly in the background, something by Patsy Cline. He backed away from the bar, pounded his chest with both his fists—*bud-a-bum*—and then stepped back up to the bar and asked Kate for a beer and a shot of whiskey. "Heh-heh-heh!!" he said. "Hey Kate . . . How 'bout a whiskeyandabeer?!" Kate wiped the bar top down with a wet rag and smiled.

"You got it, Mr. Willie," she said lovingly, like he might have been a relative. Willie Beck looked back toward the pool table at me and Larry, standing there staring at him.

"Heh-heh-heh!" he halfway screamed. "HEY!!! I'LLPLAYTHE WINNER!" he shouted with all the enthusiasm of a child, hopping on over.

"What's your name?" I asked him, holding out my hand. He took off his baseball cap and ran his hand through a sparsely populated, sweaty head of hair. He whipped the hat back on and grabbed my hand before I could take it back.

"Ask him," he said, secretively, nodding at Larry.

"Willie Beck," Larry said, pausing, looking me. "What's your name?"

"Ollie," I said, stuck in that greasy death-grip.

"Ollie, this is Willie Beck."

Willie Beck spoke like a standard transmission being driven badly, all stops and starts and hiccups. He was on some sort of natural speed, always rambling half-incoherently and bouncing around whatever room he was in like a lopsided beach ball. His clothes had a thrift-store look about them. It could have very well been that he bought his clothes at a thrift store, a Salvation Army or someplace like that—a church-basement-goodwill auction—but having met him, I'll tell you I think he earned that well-worn look honestly—greasy pit-stains and frayed pant cuffs, shoes so old they'd lost their smell and a crusty baseball cap with the Badlands Saloon logo on it. The clothes had taken on the idiosyncrasies of his body by the time our paths had crossed. He was wearing a short-sleeved yellow poly-ester shirt that might've started out all tucked in and nice, but you couldn't tell that by eight o'clock on a Saturday night. The shirt was sweat-stained, and his brown polyester pants clung to his hips for dear life, clawing against gravity and girth like two starving, wrinkled brown men hanging from a cliff.

Willie Beck lived with his brother, Llewelyn, in a crappy little alu-minum trailer next door to Wigwam just outside of Marysville. He and his brother had always lived together except for when Llewelyn signed up to fight Hitler in World War II. Aside from that, they'd always kept each other company. His brother was a quiet man. He was competent, but just this side of retarded. Their mama always told them that Willie was the smart one, that's just how it was, and they both believed her. When the war was over and things settled down a bit, Llewelyn went back to Marysville and took a job tearing tickets and cleaning up at the amphitheater in the summertime. Winter-times, he took odd jobs watching retirees' houses while they sat in the sun down in Arizona or Florida. Or he shoveled sidewalks, ran errands for the grocer, things like that. Llewelyn was the trustworthy one. That's what their mama always said.

Willie was the rambunctious one. He never made his bed and his wardrobe, as it stood, was only just barely passable. But Willie couldn't have cared less. He was so high on simply being alive 95 percent of the time that he couldn't have given a damn. Each after-noon Willie Beck left their trailer and walked the mile or so into Marysville, to the Badlands Saloon.

I've always been drawn to those characters on the sidelines—the outsiders—that little fat kid on the playground who nobody talks to, those shadows who inspire rumors. My dad's Uncle Charlie fell into this category. Charlie *was* retarded, had spent a little time at the state mental hospital in Jamestown in the 1950s. When the doctors asked him how he felt Charlie said, "Laughy-spitty," a perfect description of that place just the other side of everything making sense. When Charlie was a young man my dad saw him punch a hole through a garage door, out of rage or confusion or both. It took some pretty dark times for Charlie's parents to make the drive over to Jamestown, where the hospital was, where Charlie could get checked out and sedated. All the time I knew him he was like a mumbling/giggling teddy bear, big round belly with fat suspenders that barely held up his pants. He had big, thick, square glasses that were fingerprinted and smudgy most of the time, like his head must have been on the inside, a confirmation for him on some level that things were really just as unclear in the outside world as they were in his own head.

After my grandpa died, my grandma looked in on Charlie a cou-ple of times a week and basically became his guardian angel. He lived alone, cooked and cleaned for himself in simple ways—even made lutefisk for himself on the holidays—but he still needed a mild minder. When I was eight or ten years old I'd ride my bike over to Charlie's apartment in Bismarck and spend time with him. His apartment building was one of those generic modular buildings with twenty or thirty identical apartments, and the hallways always smelled like somebody was boiling potatoes and the televisions in all

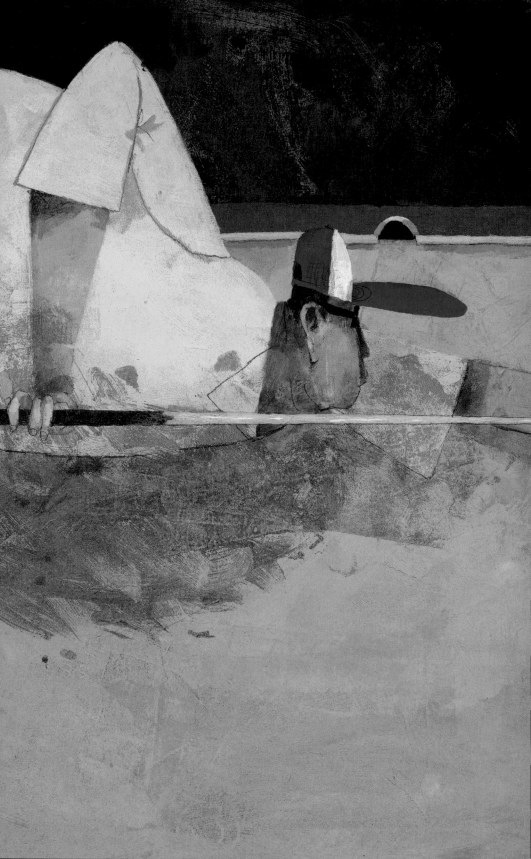

the apartments were always on. Charlie wasn't a conversationalist. I'd just sit on his green sofa and he'd sit in his junior recliner and we'd watch *Mr. Rogers' Neighborhood* or *Sesame Street*.

Willie Beck was sort of a philosophical version of my dad's retarded Uncle Charlie, except Willie wasn't retarded, just a peripheral player in a centralized world.

Willie Beck spent the majority of his life disassociated from the run-of-the-mill. He had a sort of anti-look, a gaze that never really stared back at you, eyes hidden behind old foggy prescription glasses. Willie Beck was a hard man to peg. He lived well outside the social norms of small-town life—he didn't borrow cups of sugar from his neighbors, didn't go to church, didn't shop or bathe on a regular basis. Maybe a person's life is foreshadowed by how he's put together, the quirks and intricacies—maybe a personality indelibly paves the road of a life. There's a chicken/egg aspect to this proposition, but in Willie Beck's case I think it held true: Willie Beck lived in a vacuum that went with him like an aura, a cloudy atmosphere, like he was his own planet.

That first Saturday night at the Badlands Saloon I played pool with Willie Beck, and he turned the game into a real physical sport, leaping and lunging around the table every time he'd hit the cue ball, whooping and hollering things like "HEH-HEH-HEH!!!" and "WWWHHHHOOOOOOOOOOAAAAAAA!!!" guiding the cracked balls around the green with some kind of magic that he seemed to really believe in.

After a few games and a few beers Willie Beck grabbed me and Larry around the waists—one of us on either side of him—and he told us, "Heh-heh . . . ILOVEYOUGUYS." He took off his blue, sweat-stained Badlands Saloon baseball cap and slapped it onto my head.

"Ah no, Willie, that's *your* hat," I said, uncomfortably.

"HEH-HEH," he said. "WE'LLPLAYANOTHERGAMELATER." He bounced over to the bar and ordered another drink. I took the hat off and looked at it, and then I put it back on. It was wet with Willie Beck's sweat and it was nasty, but it seemed like it would have been bad manners not to wear the damned thing.

The Mirror After Midnight

WHO YOU BE THIS EVENIN'? (heh-heh.) GOOD MORNING??? (ha!) sweet mary's ass my head hurts. what time is it? huh? i took my watch off. who turned on the shower? i think i'm looking at a mirror now. yes? yes. that's me. i gave my hat away tonight I think to a young friend. friends are good. i like friends. where'd he come from? WHERE'D I COME FROM? (heh-heh.) my hair is a little bit greasy. sweat, i s'pose. everybody's always laughed at me and my looks. i should shower more often. (heh-heh.) made me sad back then, when I was a kid and they'd laugh. i didn't understand it. I DON'T UNDERSTAND IT NOW! (heh-heh.) those were good days, though. i liked school. just wasn't any good at it. but i liked it. my glasses are old. sometimes it's blurry when i take them off and sometimes it's not. HEH!! my eyes have the veins tonight. how many nights have i been doing this? how old am i? sometimes i forget. i wish momma was still alive. i feel alone ever since she went into the ground. i helped her there. why is that so hard? why do i always have to think about it? i should have read more philosophy in school. the greeks and them. i wasn't good at school. well-behaved, but not any good. too many words in too many books. (heh-heh.) it's steamy in here now. who turned on the shower? i s'pose i did. i don't look too hot in my underwear without my glasses. even i can see that.

why is it so hard sometimes? i've got it good, you know? but it's still so hard sometimes. llewelyn doesn't ever do the dishes, and a lot of the time i don't even have anybody to talk to. but those things are easy. why is it so HARD the rest of the time? boy, i shoulda gone to church more after momma died. then i'd have felt better maybe. i liked going to church with momma. didn't like getting up early in the morning, but liked it when i was all showered and clean and on my way. ON MY WAY!! (heh-heh.) i liked that. something to start from. a starting point. it was regular. i liked that it was regular. my regular things now aren't the same and i don't know why. maybe i don't believe in heaven. do i believe in heaven? YES!! i believe in heaven. i just don't know where it's at. WHERE IS IT?!? (heh-heh.) i had fun tonight. the bar was good tonight. we played cards and I shot pool before that and gave my hat away to a young feller who was nice. he beat me at pool, but it was fun. was that heaven? (heh.) i'm tired. been doing this for a lot of years. good summer times . . .

48

Lacy, Lacy, Lacy . . .

Tank Wilson came into the bike shop one afternoon later that week with his girlfriend Lacy. "Hi," I said, shaking her hand. I didn't really shake her hand, though. It was more like she took *my* hand and she really shook it, all firm and feminine—assertive. *My God, what a girl* was all I could think.

"Hello," Lacy said, looking me straight in the eyes and smiling the way I later learned she always did. It was an intoxicating smile, a smile that could bring great, powerful men to their knees.

Tank had mentioned Lacy a few times, but it was always in passing, like she was no big deal. It might not have been wholly accurate even to describe them as "boyfriend/girlfriend" because they didn't really act that way toward each other. There was a casualness between them that was something different than the casualness between longtime lovers. There was a distance between them.

Lacy was an Indian girl—not from India, but from North Dakota. I'd never liked the term Native American because it was clunky, and I'd never heard a "Native American" refer to themselves as such, so I decided not to either. She was tall and lanky, always wore torn blue jeans and T-shirts, had long, ponytailed black hair that shined like lightning. She had a gap between her front teeth and a throaty voice and was always smiling or smirking. She made her living collecting agates at a quarry outside Marysville. She spent her afternoons there in the summertime combing through mountains of loose rocks and gravel looking for agates to sell to the guy at the roadside gas station/gift shop who, in turn, made the simple stones into key chains or little lockets. He paid Lacy by the pound for her finds and Lacy

seemed to get by. She rode a skateboard around town, which was perfect because her whole spirit just seemed to roll effortlessly along, drifting through this world without a real care at all. She was like wind and water, and she could drive a small-town kid like me mad.

"How's business?" Tank asked me, all smiles. He loved that joke, the way he'd managed to carve out this seasonal bliss for himself, a semi-career that required very little of him. I was always a little bit jealous of that quality in him, that ability to just coast along without paying life's little details any mind. Lacy was like that, too, but it was different with her. Lacy never really had anywhere that she *had* to be, and not because she was a slacker. It was something deeper with her. Lacy was *home* in Marysville, and that was enough for her, but I think Lacy could've called anyplace in the world *home*. That was just the basic connection she seemed to have with wherever she happened to be, a thousand-year-old trick that her people had learned, living out there on the prairie off the land, highly tuned-in to the gods and the Earth. Whatever it was, Lacy had it.

"So, you're livin' in New York?" Lacy asked me, casually leaning against the counter there in the shop.

"Uh, yup," I said. "Not now, of course—I'm here for the summer—but yes, I guess New York City's technically home at the moment." Lacy had a way of making me fumble for words. "Would you like a cup of coffee?" I asked her.

"YES, I WOULD," Tank bellowed from across the shop.

"Thanks," Lacy said, shaking her head at Tank's smooth belligerence. Lacy never had to ask for anything. Things just came to her.

"Anybody signed up for the ride this afternoon?" Tank asked me, walking over to the counter. "Have you taken anybody out yet this summer?" I hadn't. Tank had shown me the various routes for the guided tours around Marysville. Some of them were pretty hairy— lots of twists and turns, steep drops and narrow passes—but most of them were mapped out for amateurs, nothing dangerous or overly taxing.

"No," I said, "haven't had any takers yet this summer. But it's still June. Maybe things'll pick up around the Fourth of July."

"Maybe."

I poured two cups of coffee from the thermos there on the counter next to the cash register. Lacy took hers and sipped, staring at me with those eyes. *Was she making eyes at me, or was that just the Lacy Look?* Tank either didn't seem to notice or he didn't care. He'd probably watched her make those eyes so many times that he didn't even pay attention to them anymore. Maybe it was something that they'd both accepted about each other from the beginning: Lacy would be Tank's girlfriend, but he could never really have her all to himself.

"How's Wigwam treating you?" Lacy asked me.

"It's been great so far," I said. "Except for the mice."

Lacy just smiled. "It's quiet out there, isn't it?"

"Yes, it is," I said, looking at my shoes.

"I've spent a few nights out there," she said.

Lacy lived in a room at the Old Hotel, across the street from the Badlands Saloon. The place where she lived wasn't anything elaborate, the way everything else in Lacy's life seemed sort of transient. She was a small-town girl, but something in her soul was always on the move, like the herds of free-range bison and wild horses that roamed the Badlands, oblivious of time and space, gliding along in a world without boundaries and beyond reason.

Lacy finished her coffee and left by herself that afternoon, rolling away down Main Street on her skateboard. I watched her for a while from the large front doorway and then went back into the shop. I thought about a lot of things that summer when things got slow at Chains & Whistles, or late at night lying on the couch out at Wigwam—thought about my Bismarck past and what the future might look like; thought about drawings and paintings that I'd made, and all the pictures that were still unborn; thought about New York City and every time I did I got those butterflies I'd felt the first time I drove into the city the year before. But a lot of the time that summer, when I was all alone, it was hard not to think about Lacy.

There Is a Balm in Gilead

54 Marysville had a strange way of making you feel at home right away, like you'd been there before—maybe in another lifetime—and that was an important feeling for me to have that summer because I was a young man standing at my own personal trailhead, not so much unfolding the map of my life as I was sitting down to draw it. I'd started imagining all the choices in my life at that time as a series of swinging vines in some forest, and I was sitting on a branch of the tallest tree. That spring in New York City I didn't know what I was going to do for the summer, didn't know how I was going to pay the rent or save up enough for another expensive year in the Big Town. But somehow I never really paid any attention to basic questions like those. And it's easy not to when you're young. The trick is to keep your eyes peeled—keep your radio tuned-in and turned up— because those ropes swing back and forth in undulating rhythms and they come and go at different speeds at different times, but if you pay attention you can grab a ripe vine when it's close, in a way that makes sense. When the Marysville rope floated by I grabbed it, just like I'd grabbed the New York rope the year before.

After a couple of weeks Tank and I pretty much had everything worked out at Chains & Whistles: He'd work the morning shift— eight-till-two—and I'd pitch cleanup, closing the shop down at dusk. If anybody ever signed up for a guided ride out in the hills, Tank would watch the shop and I'd take the tour. Otherwise, I'd just make sure that the floor of the shop was well-swept and the rental bikes were in order. It was a piece of cake, really, and the hardest part was the hours and hours of nobody showing up. Next door to the shop was a portrait studio where tourists could dress up like nineteenth-century settlers, all sepia-toned and straight-faced. On the other side was the Badlands Saloon. So most of the time people just walked right past the bike shop, maybe poking their heads in long enough for me to say "Hey," but mostly not much longer than that. And that was just fine with me. I always had a sketchbook on hand to keep me busy.

Life at Wigwam was good, too. It was my first real house, on some level. I had furniture and a key to the front door. No roommates. No noisy neighbors. But the nights there scared the hell out of me because it was so damned quiet. I'd get back to Wigwam after dark most nights, or just as the sun was setting orange, make some canned supper on the stove, pop on an Otis Redding album or one by Gordon Lightfoot and eat and read and draw all by myself. *All by myself,* that was nothing new, but the silence was something I'd learned to live without.

Growing up in Bismarck, North Dakota, my greatest, most profound fear was burglars in the house, or maybe a nightmare-clown poking his head around the corner of my door frame at midnight. I could barely sleep alone when I was a child. I'd lay awake for hours back in Bismarck, underneath the covers sweating like a pig, chattering out of some primal fear of something that wasn't there. Unfortunately, that'd always been my nature.

I'd always been a bit of a spook, but I'd never lived so all alone as I was that summer in Marysville. Daytimes in the trailer were beautiful and productive, nights were nerve-racking. And there was no sense to make of it. All of my fears have always been irrational. The first time I ever slept like a baby was my first night in New York City in my crappy little dorm room at the art school, where there were no corners or closets to speak of, no hallways or hidden compartments. When I turned out the lights, some sort of night-vision allowed me to see the whole room, right there in front of me. No sudden movements. No sneak attacks.

But Wigwam was different: There was a long hallway connecting the bedroom in the back of the trailer where I was to sleep with the front living-room area, and there was just too much space there for my imagination to run wild, too many nightmare scenarios. It was all nonsense, of course, but the mind is a funny thing, especially at two o'clock in the morning in the middle of the Badlands—penetrating stars like eyes up in the sky, scavenger coyotes roaming around in the sagebrush, ghost-rocks in the moonlight forming monolithic faces. And me, there alone in an aluminum trailer, not a sound save for the mice and an occasional railroad whistle off in the distance, which only emphasized my aloneness. That first night at Wigwam, after the nervous thoughts, lying alone in the bedroom at the back of the trailer in the silence, haunted by my imagination, I gathered up the blankets and pillows and moved them out front to the couch in the living room and that's where I slept for the rest of the summer.

Everything else about Marysville felt like home, though. I had a good job and good people around me, and I had that raw country to look at, too, that landscape around Marysville in the middle of the Badlands that was so matter-of-factly majestic, like going to church every day of the week. A simple bike ride out there into those hills made you feel like Lewis and Clark, like you were seeing something for the first time, feeling something for the first time that nobody else in the whole world had ever felt before. I wondered if Willie Beck got that wild Lewis-and-Clark sensation when he looked up and out at the hills and roaming country all around him. The night he gave me his hat I took note of where he and Llewelyn lived on my way home. Their trailer looked to be in about the same condition as Wigwam—weathered and not necessarily prime real estate. Most of the trailers were for the summer employees like me, but Willie and Llewelyn lived there all year round, and had for pretty much their entire lives.

I was sitting at the bar at the Badlands Saloon on a Monday night after I'd closed down the shop, drinking dollar cans of Budweiser with Ralphy Williams, a local who everybody called Big Man because he was a massive, rugged individual—he went for something close to three hundred pounds, was married to the woman who managed Marysville's souvenir shop/bookstore, was an avid off-road biker and a big fan of Beat poetry. He was from Bozeman, Montana, a few hundred miles west on I-94. Three years earlier he'd come to Marysville to hunt white tails with some high school buddies of his when he met his wife, Glenda. He fell madly in love with her and was flooded with crazy ideas of living the simple life as a writer in the middle of the Badlands wilderness. Big Man loved Ernest Hemingway and had been working for years on a novel in the *Papa Style* and, at the time, settling down there in Marysville seemed like a perfect option. Two weeks after Big Man and Glenda met, they flew to Las Vegas and got married—quick-style—and it was the farthest either of them had ever been from home.

When they settled back down in Marysville, Glenda got Big Man a job with the Foundation, writing grants. She'd been running the little souvenir shop/bookstore for years by then, and was well-connected in a Marysville sort of way. But Big Man wanted to write his *Papa Style* novel, not pleas for money.

"A couple more?" Kate asked us as the sun was going down.

"Yes, ma'am." Big Man nodded. "So, New York City, eh?" he said, looking over at me. "Bit of a change from North Dakota, I bet." Big Man and I had met that afternoon at the bike shop. Things were slow, as usual, so we started small talking while I drew his picture.

"Yes," I said, "it's a long ways from here in a lot of different ways."

"It's funny, 'cause I couldn't wait to leave home. And then I ended up *here*," Big Man moaned, squinting into the mirror behind the bar, not really smiling.

"Yeah, but you know what," I said, "I was never really looking to escape the Midwest the way some kids are. But I guess I sure did. Things just sort of worked out the way they did, and I left."

"I hear ya," Big Man said. "There's nothing to miss around here."

"No," I said, "that's not what I mean. There's always something to miss when you leave something behind." Big Man looked at me out of the corner of his eye with an exaggerated smirk on his face, midway through a pull from his can.

"What the hell are you talking about?" he said.

I'd never had a beer before I was twenty years old, and the stuff still got on top of me pretty quickly. "Ah, you know what I mean. North Dakota is here and it's as real to me as you are sitting in front of me right now. But New York City makes sense to me, too, you know? I guess it's apples and oranges. I like both places and they both make sense."

That was the truth. *Home* is always home, and you can never really get so far away for that not to make sense. North Dakota is a wide-open place—not a lot of people and not a lot of new ideas. And back in New York I'd met a lot of people who'd been born and raised there in the same neighborhood and were working there now—had never once even left the city or sometimes not even their born-and-raised-in neighborhood. I guess in a lot of ways I saw as many similarities between New York and North Dakota as I saw differences. Because it all gets back to human nature, I suppose, and that never changes much wherever you go.

"It's been great so far," I went on. "I'm just trying to figure out how to make a living after I finish with school."

"Yeah, man, what're you gonna do?" Big Man asked me, and then he said it again: "What the hell are you gonna do?"

What was I going to do? That was a good question. But because I was on an inherently irrational adventure—*Art*—I'd never really paid that question any mind.

"I don't know. I guess I'll just draw and paint, I suppose. You know? A guy could do that, couldn't he?" Most of the time I tried to ignore that question, though, because I was still nervous in a lot of ways: *How are you going to make it, Ollie? How are you going to pay the rent/bills/bank loans, just drawing and painting, you stupid fool?* Big Man had asked the obvious question, but looking back on it now it was the wonderful thing about naive youth: Everything was so *new*, and what you hadn't learned yet you made up along the way, automatically. There's something in the brain—a buffer maybe—that never lets you fully fathom the challenges of life, never really repeats the big questions in any sort of substantial way because there are crushing possibilities. The big questions pop up like blips on a young man's mind, but are easily pushed back, to be dealt with later.

"I hear ya," Big Man continued. "But what're you gonna *do*? I mean, make pictures for magazines and stuff like that?"

"Yeah," I said, "I hope to."

"Hemingway worked as a journalist in the early years, you know."

There were half a dozen empty/slightly crushed Budweiser cans in front of us by then. It was sort of a tradition to leave the empties on the bar top when it was Dollar Bud Monday at the Badlands Saloon. Kate would just let them accumulate there like little aluminum trophies.

"How've things been going for you?" I asked Ralphy. Big Man was pretty young—about Tank Wilson's age. He had a degree from Montana State University, but he seemed stuck, like he was in a rut. He paused when I asked him the question, drank an entire can of beer and then just laughed out loud the way only a man his size can, big and full of irony.

"Man, I'm counting down the days until I can get outta here." He accepted another round of beers. "I'm doing pretty good, all in all," he said. "I'm just restless, I guess, but it's summertime here now and that's a good thing. You've never been here in the winter, have you?"

"No."

"Well, that's a whole different horse, winters up here. Any sense of isolation you have here in the summertimes, multiply that by the biggest number you can imagine and that's nearly how bad it is here, come December or January or February. In a lot of ways, February is the worst. I don't know what it is, but I feel like a god-damned wild animal by the time February rolls around. I feel like an inmate here, when the wintertime peaks. Jesus, it's just a hellish thing. And there's not enough beer or whiskey in the world to take that dreadful feeling away. I've tried, man. Believe me, I've tried. But nothing works when it's cold and empty in Marysville."

Several hours had passed and the bar was getting full. The musical had ended up at the amphitheater and the actors and tourists were winding their ways back down into Marysville, to the bars and the restaurants, and to the Badlands Saloon.

"How meenie beers we've had, anyway?" I asked Big Man. My tongue was kind of numb. Big Man had been ordering dollar beers faster than I could comfortably drink them, and Big Man could comfortably drink about anybody underneath the table. I was young and inexperienced and when a guy gets to talking while he's drinking, time and count can slip away from him. "YeeeAAHHHH!" I hollered a little too loud the next time Kate came around to offer us another couple of beers. "TWOMORE!" I slurred at her, smiling. The juke-box had been turned on and was quietly building speed. "ILOVE-JOHNNYCASH!" I screamed emphatically at Big Man and pounded the top of the bar with my fist. He crushed another can and patted me on the shoulder.

"I love Johnny Cash, too, man," he said. He seemed like he was so sober just then, like a big rugby saint or something. He sat there drinking calmly, because he was a lot bigger than me and had been

through this all maybe a million times before. Big Man had been ordering rounds at his leisure up until then, not really paying attention to my increasing drunkenness. "How you doin'?" he asked me. "Feelin' okay?"

Part of my mind knew what the real question was: *You're getting good and drunk, aren't you, my lightweight friend?* And I was, but that wasn't altogether fair. I was feeling *alive*, too. "YEAHBIGMAN!" I hollered out, offering my beer can high in the air for a toast. I was sitting on the stool at the bar closest to the front door and Big Man was sitting next to me. "CHEEEEEEERRRSS!!" I shouted. It wasn't necessary to scream at that point and I knew it, but what the hell. When you're there—getting high—negative thoughts can't matter. It was all *Happy Time.*

Kate came by and asked if we'd have two more and I answered loudly, with all sorts of enthusiasm—"YESGODDAMNITWE'LLAB-SOLUTELYDEFINITELYHAVEACOUPLEMOREKATEYOUBEAU-TIFULWONDERFULBLACKVESTEDANGELCHILD!!!!"

Whoa. All of my words were running together and my volume control was broken. I was really lit up. Big Man was just trying to enjoy himself, trying to forget about all the isolation he was feeling for a little while, but I was well on my way to some serious life lessons. I'd never been much of a drinker, and I don't really know why. Every high school kid in North Dakota—especially out in the country, where there wasn't much for hormone-crazed kids to do—spent some considerable time sampling various beers and schnapps, discovering those inevitable boundaries, throwing up at proms or in the backseats of their girlfriends' fathers' cars. But I'd never really run down that road. I'd never even stuck a thumb out there, and I don't really know why that was. I wasn't exactly general circulation in high school, wasn't the go-to guy. I was a peripheral player too, I guess, kind of like Willie Beck in a real roundabout way. I had my few friends back then and that seemed to be about enough for me at the time.

I'd always been a momma's boy, too. I never did anything that I couldn't look my mom in the eyes and tell her about. That's just how I was. Some genetically innocent thing about *Pride* or *Honor.* No booze or cigarettes or anything that would make my sweet mother shake her head in shame. So while the majority of my classmates in high school were out and about experimenting and pushing on those boundaries, I was holed-up in my dad's studio, painting or drawing. Painting and drawing—those seemed like safe enough things for me at the time, places where I couldn't get into any real sort of trouble, places where mistakes were welcomed.

Kate came down to our end of the bar asking if we'd have another round, but Big Man drew two fingers across his throat, nodding in my direction and shaking his head. There were eighteen or twenty empty cans of beer on the bar in front of us, and two or three full ones in front of me, warm now, their pop-tops pointing up toward the ceiling of that beautiful barroom, saluting me.

"ISSSSSGOOOOOODDTIMMMESNOW, EH!?" I hollered/slurred over at Big Man. It must've been about midnight by then and we'd been nursing our way along for hours. Big Man was a little bit drunk too, I think, but not like me.

"ILOOOOOVETHISSONG!" I screamed. The great old Bob Seger song—"Against the Wind"—came rolling out of the jukebox speakers with that steady, sure rhythm. God did I love that song. It was one of those songs that seemed damned-near religious in the smoky late-night ambiance of the Badlands Saloon. *We were young and strong / we were runnin' / Against the wind . . .* Jesus yes. That's how I felt then, in the drunken dawn of my summer there in Marysville, smack-dab in the middle of the Badlands, without a clue and without a concern. Big Man was getting a little blurry by then, and it wasn't his fault. My vision was going to the dogs.

"OKAYMYMAN!!" I screamed. "TIMEFORBEDIGUESS."

Big Man paid for the beers because I couldn't find my wallet, but it didn't matter to me then. *Finders keepers,* I figured. I waved to Kate behind the bar, blew her a kiss and staggered out of the Badlands Saloon. *It's all just a dream anyway.*

My bike was still leaning against the front of the building outside, just like Tank Wilson had told me it always would be. I was wobbly as hell and straddling the bike was a chore in and of itself. I shoved off and rolled down the main street of that sleepy little Midwestern town. The air was cool and the street was empty. I coasted the few blocks to the edge of town and down the road that ran out toward the trailer park. The streetlights disappeared behind me and the stars and a full moon were out in full force up above and I looked up

to see them and it was incredible, all those little pinholes of light hypnotizing me, the moon a holy coin stuck up there against a soft/dark cathedral sky. I saw a shooting star and then a satellite blipping along. *I betcha that thing is really moving,* I said out loud to myself. I stared up at the star-spangled sky for a long time, coasting down that midnight road, and when I looked back down at the pavement the whole world started to tip over. I spilled across the shoulder of the road and crashed down into the ditch into a soft pile of tumbleweeds, my orange bike all tangled up with my legs. I laughed for a long time, staring up at the stars and winking. I staggered back to my feet and started rolling again, still laughing to myself in the pitch-black Badlands.

When I got to the little gravel road that lead to the trailer park I stopped and stood there in the pitch blackness. Across the way—opposite the trailer park road—was the curving paved road that led up to the amphitheater where they had the musical every night all summer long. *I should see that place,* I said to myself. *Especially right now. I bet it's pretty in the moonlight.*

I crossed the road and headed up toward the amphitheater. It was a steep hill in places and the road twisted back and forth as I climbed. I had to walk my bike most of the way because my energy was low even though my spirits were higher than the hills. I crested the top of the hill and rolled my bike through the gravel parking lot there, and then on to a little grassy area in front of the ticket booth. The moon was nearly full and I could see everything in a bone-glow light: The parking lot, the ticket booth and beyond, down some stairs and an escalator, the hi-tech amphitheater with hundreds of empty seats, the stage and the speakers and the lights, all quiet now. You could almost hear the moon buzzing up there in the sky. Beyond the amphitheater the Badlands sprawled out like an African landscape, silent-strength manifest.

It was a strange feeling looking out on those hills and intermittent flatlands, a feeling of loneliness and fear and euphoria all at the same time, like snorkeling in the ocean and all of a sudden the ocean floor disappears and there you are, just floating above an incomprehensible darkness. It's a terrifying feeling of flying, but there's a peacefulness in it, too, when that realization hits you that you're no more than a single drop of rainwater in that ocean—

maybe even less—but you're alive there, right there at that moment, in spite of the odds, you're alive.

There was a bench in front of the ticket booth that I'd been leaning against. I sat down and rested my head in my hands, then sort of leaned over. I thought about my mom and my dad and my little brother back in Bismarck. I thought about New York City and wondered if it could ever get as quiet there as those Badlands were in the moonlight. Then I lay down on that bench and fell asleep.

I woke up to the sound of church music. I was lying on my side with my eyes closed. It was the old hymn "There Is a Balm in Gilead," sung all choppy and full of quavering vibrato by some unaccompanied group of people who for some godforsaken reason seemed to be all around me at that moment. The song was familiar to me, but the version this a cappella choir was singing seemed foreign under the circumstances. There was a sensational light flooding through the lids of my eyes and my mouth was dry and seemed to be glued shut, and an almost frightening pain in my brain, a general hurt that was so vast and dominant that I just lay there paralyzed for another minute or two. The choir hit the second verse and I got emotional. I cracked open one eye with great difficulty. I was still lying on the bench I'd found in the moonlight the night before, but it wasn't just a regular bench. It was a pew.

I sat up very slowly. It turned out I was in the third row of about a dozen church pews, set up for open-air morning Lutheran church services up there outside the amphitheater. It was Tuesday, the best I could remember. *Why the church service? Why now? Why here, on top of a grassy plateau with aerial views of Marysville and all the hills for miles and miles in any direction?* It was a beautiful place to worship—no doubt about that—but please, God, *why now?* There were forty or fifty people in the pews around me and a casually dressed pastor up in front of the rows of pews leading everybody in song. The pastor was dressed comfortably, like everybody else, his shirt tucked into fresh-pressed khakis, a wedding ring shining in the morning sun on his left hand. I looked to my left at an elderly tourist couple sitting there singing, both of them dressed in shorts and sandals and tourist hats. I looked to my right at a nice little family of four. The young boy there—his hair still damp and combed over tightly—looked up at me and I would have smiled at him but I felt like I was watching a movie that I didn't want to be in. He seemed a little bit nervous, too. He wasn't used to spending Tuesday mornings in church and quite frankly, neither was I. And this little boy surely wasn't used to corpses like me rising up in the pew next to him, all cotton-mouthed, in a state of temporary death.

Nobody else seemed to pay me any mind, though, so I decided to stand up. *Where's my bike?* I thought to myself. And then a sensation I'd never really experienced before hit me, a strange lurching movement in my gut, a violent roiling of my insides like there was a cat and a dog in there somewhere, wrestling over rat meat. I grabbed the pew in front of me and half buckled over, the feeling damned-near knocking me out. I took my hat off because I'd started to sweat like a maniac and I looked up at the pastor, singing all full-voiced, waving his hands, keeping time for the congregation. He saw me standing there, half buckled over and smiled happily, like I was just another member of the flock. And indeed I was, but I needed some serious heavenly intervention. I started to smile, and then I threw up in my hat.

I was as surprised as anyone. I'd never felt like that before. There was absolutely no communication between my stomach and my brain. It was all I could do to get my hat up in time to protect those poor tourists sitting in the pew in front of me from a hellish morning bath. It wasn't a picnic for me, and once it was all in my hat, it was over, like Old Faithful pouring forth, and then just the silence.

The pastor seemed to be about the only person who even really noticed. The pastor and that poor little boy sitting next to me, who would probably never be the same again. I was in shock and just shrugged at him, dazed, my eyes wide, wiping the corners of my mouth on the sleeves of my T-shirt, trying to balance the pool in my hat. I slipped out of the pew as the congregation was wrapping up the song: *"There is a balm in Gilead to make the wounded whole; there is a balm in Gilead to heal the sin-sick soul."*

Please God, lead me to that balm, I said to myself as I left. I found my bike and headed back down the hill toward Wigwam. It'd been a long night and I needed a shower.

Walking Every Day

The ride down the hill from the amphitheater was nearly as hard as the ride up had been the night before. My headache had eased a bit, but I could still just barely keep my eyes open against the strong morning sunshine. At the bottom of the hill I passed Willie Beck, out for a morning walk. "Hey-yup," he said, not really looking at me, waving his arm in the air as I passed by. Willie Beck was sort of a power-walker, really rambling along—arms all waving and legs really moving—but not for any physical fitness sort of reason. He just walked like that—sober or otherwise—one foot in front of the other, always a different foot-fall, lots of body motion, deeply into the walk.

•   •   •

(heh-heh.) that's the new guy. good guy. we had fun the other night. did I give him my hat? think I did. too much beer that night. too much beer last night by the looks of him. (heh-heh.) good guy, though, good guy. tall guy. must be a good six and a half feet tall. pretty good pool player. skinny, too. i ain't never been tall. never been skinny, neither. (heh-heh.) nice day today. nice day yesterday. always nice in the summertime. gettin' too old for the cold. gettin' too old for the cold. but where would i go anyway? no place to go to. just right here. too old to go anywhere anyway. llewelyn was still sleeping when i left. llewelyn, he sleeps a lot. always has. sometimes i can't sleep that much. always fall asleep easy. then i get up easy, too. (heh.) i like walkin'. it's easy. good to get out of the house. maybe go to the grocery store today. yes? i don't know. we got pretty good food back at the trailer. maybe i'll go to the store tomorrow. will walk again tomorrow. i like walking.

•   •   •

I rinsed my hat out with a garden hose back at Wigwam and set it out to dry on the front steps. I went inside and drank half a glass of tap water. It tasted like blood, but it wasn't so bad because it was wet and I was dry. The cats and dogs were at it again in my gut, but there wasn't much left down there to fight over. I peeled down and stepped into the narrow shower at the back of the trailer toward the bedroom that I hadn't been sleeping in. It was a hell of a way to start a Tuesday, throwing up in my hat in the middle of "There Is a Balm in Gilead." Jesus, if they could see me now back in Bismarck. My mom would never forgive me, but my mom would never know.

I dried off and walked back out into the little living room and very gently laid down on the couch. My headache was still pounding, but it was bearable. I even smiled a little bit to myself, because it had been a fun night. Big Man was a good guy. I'd never out-drink him, but I still looked forward to spending some more time with him. He seemed like a drifter, too, just like me except for a whole different set of reasons. I think that when he was living in Bozeman he was watching the vines, too, only the vine that he grabbed swung him into a marriage and into Marysville and he was feeling a little bit dead-ended by the time I got to town. It's an inevitable feeling, I suppose—the realization that you've made a wrong turn—but that's why you have to pay attention to the vines.

As I was lying there on the couch at Wigwam I looked over randomly at the coffee table next to the sofa. My wallet was there on the coffee table, tied with a little piece of string to a note and an agate. I reached over and picked it up, untied the note and read it in the dim, late-morning light of the trailer:

"Ollie. You shouldn't leave this where other people can find it. XO Lacy."

What was this? Lacy'd obviously found my wallet at the bar, somehow, after I'd left the night before, but how the hell had she gotten into the trailer? Did she have a goddamned key or something? Or was she a locksmith, too? If Wigwam had to be burglarized by anybody, I was kind of glad that it had been Lacy. The whole idea of Lacy having been there in the trailer on that morning was an antidote to the wicked way I was feeling.

I closed my eyes. Things were starting to feel almost human again, but I needed a little rest before my shift at the bike shop so I fell asleep for an hour or so there on the couch at Wigwam as the sun climbed the sky outside, visions of Lacy dancing across my dreams.

• • •

i love walkin'. always have. it's good alone-time. (heh.) llewelyn he's my brother so i love him, but it's good to get outta the house. (heh.) what the hell is that on the road up there? looks like a lump. no, it looks like an animal. what is that? oh no. a raccoon. oh no. yikes. poor fellah's been runned over. he's smashed flat right down the middle. smashed down the middle in the middle of the road. that's something. ouch. yikes. "you okay little feller?" oh no, he's still alive. aw no. he's flat to the ground in the middle. his little paws are pawing toward the ditch. aw no. "you're still alive, fellah. but you're stuck." i'll just walk past him. poor guy. oh man. helluva way to go. must hurt. or maybe it doesn't hurt at all. he didn't say anything. will he be okay? nope. road kill when it's dead isn't a big deal—you don't even notice it most of the time—but poor little guy dying there is hard to look at. just keep walkin', that's what i'll do. i like walkin'. poor guy. poor, poor little guy. look back one more time. then just keep walkin'.

• • •

I threw on some clothes and my hat—the thing was pretty much dry, sitting out there in the sun for a few hours—and rode slowly through the trailer park, past Willie and Llewelyn's house, through the campground and down the gravel road to the main road that passed into and through Marysville. I looked up toward the amphitheater there on the hill and then just steered toward town.

Halfway down the road to Marysville I came across a God-awful sight: A poor fat raccoon, flattened out in the middle of the road. I slowed down and stopped above him. It was a fresh kill, or so I was thinking when the little soul raised a shaking paw and slowly blinked up at me. The sad creature was still alive, somehow, even with its body smashed all to pieces, as thin as a glove all through the middle of its wild body. *God,* I thought. *Somebody should put this thing out of its misery.* I pushed off and rode fast into town. I wasn't thinking about my own headache anymore, the rotten taste in my mouth or the pain in my eyes from the sunshine. *How should I do it?* I thought to myself. *How can I put that dying raccoon away?*

I pulled up to the shop. Tank Wilson was sitting out front in one

of the lawn chairs drinking coffee. "Mornin'," he said. "Heard you had a good night last night?"

"Yeah," I said. "You got a small two-by-four?" Tank looked up at me. "What'd'ya need that for?"

"There's a raccoon out on the road that's been run over and he's still alive. I want to put him down."

Tank didn't hesitate. He found a two-foot board under a tarp in the back corner of the shop and handed it to me. I hopped on my bike and headed back out to where the raccoon had been. I was nervous while I rode. I'd never really killed anything brutally before, like I was about to do now. I'd hunted with my dad when I was a kid back in Bismarck—birds, mostly, pheasants and grouse and partridge—and once I'd had to ring the neck of a bird that I'd only just winged, the way my dad had told me I'd have to do if I'd ever only just wounded an animal, because it was part of the deal with the bird: *"If you're going to hunt me, kill me fairly, and don't make me suffer."*

I got to the spot where the raccoon had been but he wasn't there anymore. Nothing was there—no blood or guts or skid marks. I checked the ditches on both sides of the road. Nothing. Out past the ditch a ways on one side of the road was Wallingford Creek, trickling along, and on the other side of the road grasslands, and beyond that just the hills. But no raccoon—alive or dead—anywhere in sight.

I turned around and rode back to the shop. "Did you get him?" Tank asked me. He was sitting in his lawn chair again, drinking coffee in the large, open-fronted doorway of the shop.

"No," I said. "He wasn't there."

The Jigglers

It was a little after two o'clock later that week and nobody had signed up for the afternoon ride. I wondered if anybody ever would. It seemed to me that Chains & Whistles was more of an expensive window decoration for Marysville and the summertime tourists than an actual, functioning bike shop. I popped a Cowboy Junkies tape into the boombox, sat down with a sketchbook and started doodling things the way some people keep track of their thoughts in journals and diaries. I drew a picture of Tank Wilson, and then a squashed raccoon in the middle of the road. I drew another picture of Willie Beck (I'd drawn a bunch of pictures of Willie Beck by then, all from memory because I never did get a picture of the guy). I drew a picture of Lacy and her midnight-black hair and her wicked grin. *Lacy, Lacy, Lacy.*

Three guys came strolling into the shop, hands in their pockets, in no real hurry. "Good afternoon," I said. "How's it goin'?" I vaguely recognized them from the various poster-advertisements around town for the musical up at the amphitheater. They were a juggling act from Los Angeles called the Jigglers and they were the only professional cross-dressing juggling group in the world, as far as anybody could tell. They dressed up as big bimbos each night and put on a slightly off-color show that was aimed more toward the fraternity crowd than the North Dakota tourist trade. But they'd been offered the half-time gig at the musical that summer and the money was too good to pass up.

"You guys are performing up at the amphitheater, right?"

"Yeah, that's us." Hokey Carmichael was the group's leader—a stout, hard-drinking, hard-smoking comedian who looked like hell in nylon stockings and flip-flops, the dark cartoon-character of the bunch. Hank Langhorne and Fritz—the other two Jigglers—didn't say much, standing there in the massive front doorway of Chains & Whistles, a classic offstage presence, I suppose, for those who yuk it up every night. The Jigglers had a definite performer's odor about them, too, somewhere in between New York City homeless and caged lemur. And they looked like fools when they got all made up for the show each night—wigs and skirts and massive, inflatable fake breasts. Tank had seen their show and said they were hysterical, but that there seemed to be a disconnect between them and the audiences in Marysville that summer.

Ten years earlier the Jigglers had been beach bums, Hokey told me, loafing college dropouts who spent most of their time surfing in Malibu and smoking grass. They'd had a midnight brainstorming session, he said, wading in the waves of the Pacific Ocean, concocting the most ridiculous way they could make a living. They'd considered being bank robbers or starting a pornographic Internet website, but those things seemed too conventional. All three of them were competent jugglers, but even that seemed a little bit run-of-the-mill to them at the time, standing there on the beach in Malibu at midnight, stoned and happy.

"So we pushed the juggling idea around for a couple of hours: 'Maybe we could juggle children?' 'Maybe we could be nude jugglers!' We were getting close. And then, eureka—'CROSS-DRESSING JUGGLERS!'" Hokey laughed for a second and then stopped, like there might've been a little bit of regret in him somewhere. "I think Hank had the idea, actually."

"I haven't seen the show yet, but I've heard a lot about it."

"Well, it's been a helluva deal so far," Hokey Carmichael told me. "You ever been booed by hundreds of people on a nightly basis? It's something else, I'll tell you what."

"Wow," I said. "Kind of a conservative crowd?"

"Conservative has nothing to do with it," he said. "*Geriatric* would be a better way to describe it. But what the hell can you expect from sixty-two busloads of blue-haired retirees?" I liked Hokey Carmichael. He was a no-nonsense kind of guy.

"We're just trying to avoid being the first cross-dressing juggling act to get lynched by a bunch of pensioners," Hank Langhorne chimed in.

I offered them all a cup of coffee. "No, thanks," Hokey said. "We're gonna go grab a beer next door. If you want to see the show sometime, though, let us know. We'll get you in."

"Okay."

The Jigglers were just passing through, like me, on their way to someplace else. And I'd always envied bands and guys who got to be a part of a performing group—there was something communal about it, the idea of creating something in concert with somebody else. Drawing and painting could be a lonely business.

I sat back down and started drawing again. It was an older sketchbook. I flipped through some of the earlier pages—my first days in New York City that previous fall: A picture of a man crying in a telephone booth, screaming *"I JUST CAN'T TAKE IT ANYMORE"*; a picture of a homeless man shitting on a subway grate; a police officer in Washington Square Park; a Gandhi statue in Union Square; a pretty girl with rollerblades at a Barnes & Noble bookstore. Drawings are funny, because when you look at them later you remember exactly where you were when you drew them, the way the weather was, what people around you were saying at the time. It's almost like the act of drawing itself burns the memory into your mind, a split-second event where your senses are all cranked up to their highest levels and everything is crystal clear, like remembering the second you were born, a vivid memory of what coming into this life felt like.

Happy Trails

The atmosphere at Chains & Whistles was sleepy that summer, the days just drifting along. Tank and I were sitting there in our late-June lawn chairs one afternoon drinking coffee when a family came into the shop. "Good afternoon," the father said. "How are you men doing?"

"Swell," Tank said, looking up from his lawn chair.

The family was a pretty standard Midwestern bunch, pleasant and friendly, all smiles. Except for the father. The father had a severe military crew cut and a tattoo of a dying swan and the words *"Never Forget"* on his right bicep. He clearly spent a lot of time doing push-ups and when he smiled it wasn't so much a smile as a flash of gritted teeth. The rest of the family looked like they might've been a little bit afraid of him.

"Ollie," I said, holding a hand out to the father.

"Colonel James Lawrence," he said, grabbing my hand and nearly breaking it. "This is my wife Gloria. That's Debra," he said, pointing to the girl. He looked at the little boy: "Tell the man your name, son."

"Billy," the boy said quietly.

"The boy's name is William," Colonel James Lawrence said to me and flashed his teeth.

All four of them were wearing matching T-shirts with brown stripes—casual summer uniforms, like they were a vacationing militia group. The girl was at that tall and gangly phase of her life. The little boy was younger, nine or ten years old. "We're interested in renting four bikes and taking a tour," the father said, clenching his teeth and smiling.

"Sure," Tank said. "Ollie?" Tank looked over at me with that rye-whiskey twinkle in his eyes.

"Okay," I said. "Let's go for a ride."

Tank sized the family up and pulled four bikes down off the racks. "Why don't you find them some helmets," he said to me as he checked over the bikes. I walked over to the big box in the middle of the shop where we kept all the head gear, set the kids up and handed one to Gloria, the wife. She smiled and said, "Thank you." I tried to give a helmet to Colonel James Lawrence.

"No thanks, Private. I'm not wearin' one," he said. I told him that we were required to fit everybody with helmets, but he wasn't having it.

"There ain't nothin' out there that's gonna hurt this man," he said, flashed some teeth and turned to get his bike. The mother looked at me and smiled, and that was that.

I hadn't taken anybody out for a ride yet that summer so I had the butterflies a little bit, a virgin mountain bike tour guide. We saddled the Lawrences up and headed out, south out of town on a gravel road that climbed the southern lip of the bowl that Marysville sat in.

"Where are you from?" I asked the Colonel as we rode along.

"Grand Forks," he said. "You know where that is, don't you, Private?" He was really working at the climb, standing up in the saddle, flexing his muscles and grinding his teeth. I did know where Grand Forks was, tucked up in the extreme northeastern corner of the state. There was an Air Force base there, so I assumed the Colonel was a military man. He certainly had the grit. There were a lot of guys like the Colonel in North Dakota, actually, because there were a lot of military bases in North Dakota. At one time, had North Dakota seceded from the Union it would've been the third-largest nuclear power in the world behind the rest of the States and the Soviets. That's something to think about. A little bit cynical, too—I guess the boys in Washington figured that if our nuclear arsenal were to be attacked, a wide-open, thinly populated place like North Dakota would make for a good fallout zone. And with a couple thousand Colonel James Lawrences peppered across the state, when the going got tough, the tough would be there to flex their muscles and snarl.

Gloria Lawrence and Debra and little Billy were slow on the climb, so the Colonel and I stopped as we crested the hill and waited for them to catch up. The Colonel inhaled the fresh Badlands after-

noon air deeply through his nose and then blew it out fast. "Good day for a workout," he said.

When Gloria and the kids caught up to us, Gloria was panting. "There aren't too many climbs out there where I'll be taking you guys today," I told them. She was a little heavy in the middle—a classic Midwestern prosperity—and the hill had been workout enough for her at that point. "I'll take you on the Snake Trail," I said and little Billy looked up at me quickly, all panicky.

"Why do they call it that?" he asked me nervously.

"Oh, don't worry," I said, trying to reassure the poor boy. "The trail twists back and forth a lot, like the shape of a snake. That's why they call it the Snake Trail." He was a quiet and shy child, seemed like he was easily intimidated. "You'll do great, I can tell already," I told him. He smiled weakly and looked up at his father. "There are some beautiful views out there where we're going," I told them.

Just over the top of the hill we left the gravel road and crossed over a ditch. There was a barbed-wire fence and a rickety old wooden gate. I got off my bike, opened the gate and let everyone through. They all had super-serious looks on their faces, like we were really going on an adventure.

Just inside the fence there was a single-track dirt trail that would take us—snaking—east to west, dropping us out on the other side of the amphitheater. It was a nice ride and I never tired that whole summer long of getting out there into that open country, so silent and majestic—just the sound of the wind rushing past your ears— and being up on a plateau, as we were, you could see for a hundred miles. The sky itself even looked bigger with a view like that, and the hills and grasslands that rolled out to the horizon were like great paintings, almost abstract in their vastness.

I took the lead and we zipped down into a narrow alleyway between two rock walls. The Colonel flew in behind me, keeping his front tire two or three inches from mine, as if to say: *Give it to me, Private, because I can take it.* I tried to keep the pace casual, but the Colonel really wanted to go. After a mile or so, I looked back and asked how everyone was doing.

"WE'RE DOING GREAT, PRIVATE!" the Colonel hollered. Gloria and the kids were twenty-five or thirty yards behind me and the Colonel so I pulled over to let them catch up.

"What's the holdup?" the Colonel asked me. He was all red and sweating, veins popping out in his head, smiling that teeth-gritted smile of his.

"Let's wait for the others to catch up," I said.

"Don't you worry about them, Private." He looked over his shoulder and screamed: "LET'S DOUBLE-TIME IT BACK THERE!"

Everybody fell in and we carried on like that, like an accordion, expanding and contracting, the Colonel making the ride a life-or-death race, the other three—Gloria, Debra and little Billy Lawrence—doing their best to keep up.

We came to a smooth straightaway in the trail and I opened it up a bit, pedaled a few times hard and then just hunkered down over the handlebars for a little blast. The Colonel was right on top of me, of course, so I pumped the bike a few more times and really got things going.

The trail dipped down toward the end of the straightaway and then hopped back up onto a flat tabletop of dirt and rock. I caught the edge of this tabletop and pulled up and pedaled once hard— just at the right moment—and floated for a while through the air. In the flash of time I was airborne I looked down and caught a glimpse of a coiled thing the size of a small car tire. I knew in an instant what it was because it was the only thing I was ever truly afraid of when I'd ride off-road in the Badlands: A snake.

I glanced back to see the thing strike the back part of the Colonel's bike frame as he passed over it. It struck at him and then recoiled and hissed ferociously. I'd pulled over and was trying to warn the rest of the family before they caught up to me and the Colonel.

"Careful, Colonel," I said, waving my arms, trying to get Gloria's attention. But it was too late—Gloria and the kids were already rolling up to the tabletop. Debra was in the lead, and as she rode up toward me and the Colonel the snake hissed at her and lunged. She screamed hysterically, leaping off her bike and letting it fall. Gloria looked up to see what was going on.

"A SNAKE!" Debra wailed, running over to her father. Little Billy peeked out from behind his mother with terror in his eyes.

"Is that a rattlesnake?!" Debra shrieked.

"Christ no," the Colonel told her. "That's just a pissed-off bull snake."

The Colonel set his bike down very carefully and assumed a martial arts stance. He marched confidently over to the snake, spread his legs and leaned over it. The snake hissed a warning and lunged at the Colonel's left leg. Like a panther the Colonel hopped to the right, grabbed the snake by its tail in a single movement and started swinging it around in the air like a lasso, around and around, faster and faster until the reptile was just a blur. Debra was screaming and little Billy started to cry. The Colonel cranked the snake around a couple of more times to reach some sort of crazy critical velocity and then he cracked the animal's head down onto the rock of the tabletop like it was a bullwhip. He smacked the animal down with such force that the thing nearly broke in two. He tossed the carcass off into some weeds and got back onto his bicycle.

"Let's go, Private." The Colonel acted like nothing had happened. He didn't need a helmet. He was a soldier.

Dark storm clouds had been rolling in as we rode and the air was still, like before a thunderstorm. Gloria and the kids were behind us a ways again, crying and moaning. "We're gonna get some rain," I told the Colonel. "Maybe we should double back to the shop."

"Nonsense," he said.

So we pushed on. The Snake Trail was a particularly beautiful ride—nothing too challenging, just a nice smooth ride through canyons and past streams and wildflowers. But the day had turned into something else altogether. There was a gloom in the air now, figuratively and literally. It hadn't rained much that summer, but the storm clouds were upon us now and it was nearly dark out there on the trail. "I think we're gonna get wet, Colonel," I said, and the rain started coming down. It wasn't a gradual sprinkle, either. God turned the faucet on and the water started coming down immediately in a flood, like we were riding along on the floor of an ocean.

"Dad!" little Billy called out from somewhere behind us.

"STEP IT UP, WILLIAM. LET'S GO!"

Billy started crying again and the Colonel scolded him.

"HE'S JUST A BOY, JIM!" Gloria screamed through the water.

"NO HE'S NOT!" the Colonel bellowed back. "HE'S WEAK!"

I let the Colonel go on ahead and dropped back in with Gloria and the kids. "It'll be all right," I told them. "We're almost there."

By the time we got back to the shop we looked like refugees from some forgotten war, wet and forlorn. "Got a little bath, huh," Tank said, like it was a joke.

We found some towels and dried off. The Colonel paid us and Tank took their four bikes back into the work area to clean them up. Gloria looked frustrated, like they'd all been through this storm a million times before. Little Billy and Debra were still crying quietly.

"Thanks for the ride, Private," the Colonel said and pounded me on the back. "That was fun."

The Games We Play

90   *OH WE'RE REALLY MOVING NOW! gin rummy. fun game. funny game. same game every time with a different winner. i don't win too much and i don't even care, neither. (heh.) i saw a picture of the queen once. where's she live again? don't know. don't care. llewelyn was a bastard last night. used up all the hot water. never saw a picture of the king, though. who's the king? where's he live? (heh-heh.) need 'nother drink. whiskey? beer? yes. yes all. who's that? jimmy threepence comin' in. what a talker. he talks too much. always always always talking talking talking. what an accent. don't even notice it anymore, though, i s'pose. jimmy threepence talks like the queen but not as good. i never heard the king talk. is there a king? who picks the kings and the queens and the jacks? what about the numbers? my daddy always said that we're born with one set of numbers and we spend the rest of our lives waitin' on the other ones. for the rock on the grave i s'pose. this to that. and then a name, and then a funny little sentence out of a children's book. that's the last thing i need, another set of numbers. jimmythreepence-jimmythree-pence-jimmythreepence. he makes you want to say his name three times. (heh-heh.) his name makes you want to tell him to shut the hell up. he talks too much, too much. llewelyn talks too much, too. but he's my brother. everybody talks too much sometimes. sometimes all the time. (heh-heh.)*

· · ·

Willie Beck and I had started talking quite a bit when our paths would cross around town. I saw him a lot in the mornings and in the afternoons when I was coming and going to and from Wigwam and I'd usually stop and talk with him for a while when he was sitting out in front of his trailer. That whole summer I never once met Willie Beck's brother, Llewelyn, but Willie usually filled me in anyway, complained about the little things his brother had or hadn't done that bothered him, the same way anybody would do. Willie Beck was a funny conversationalist, too—he sort of rambled between total incoherency and jaw-dropping, almost prophetic clarity. Willie had a way of boiling down the most complicated things in the world to utter simplicity. Like the time I'd asked him if he'd seen anybody hanging around Wigwam—I'd told him about my wallet and how Lacy had somehow gotten into the trailer to return it. I'd told him it was an awkward situation because I worked for Tank and he and Lacy were some sort of a couple, but Willie just laughed at that and stuttered and told me, straight as an arrow: "Doesn't sound like a problem to me. Sounds like fun."

June was wearing thin. I was talking with Kate at the bar, doing a bit of socializing because there wasn't much of it going on at Chains & Whistles. The musical was winding down up at the amphitheater and everybody was heading back down into town. Jimmy Threepence walked into the bar. Jimmy Threepence talked constantly, even if nobody was listening, and usually they weren't. He was born and raised in Marysville—had never left, hadn't even been to Dickinson, the next biggest town just east of Marysville on Interstate 94. Jimmy Threepence was a midget, or a *Little Person*—or *Height Challenged*—I'm not sure how to properly describe his condition but he was barely four feet tall, maybe even less. He was certifiably short, about Willie Beck's age—I think they'd gone to school together— and he spoke with a thick, affected English accent, even though his parents were born-and-bred North Dakotans, through and through.

"What's the deal with his accent?" I asked Kate from across the bar. The Badlands Saloon was pretty-well full—music and laughter and smoke and people—most of the regulars were there, a few tourists and a handful of the performers from up at the musical. Most of the tourists and performers generally hung out at the other bar in Marysville, a slightly more contemporary sort of place with a blackjack table, a digital jukebox and a full kitchen. The mayor— Donald Grinhauser—and other city officials tended to hang out at that bar, too. It was a cleaner place, closer to the main road running through Marysville out to the Interstate and more popular with the tourists, which is probably why the politicians spent more time there. I preferred the Badlands Saloon.

"Oh, Jimmy's funny," Kate said, "he's been around forever. He actually used to baby-sit me when I was two or three years old," she said. "My parents went to school with him." There was an image: The midget Jimmy Threepence babysitting an infant girl who was nearly half as tall as him straight out of the womb. Maybe that's where the accent came from, maybe Jimmy just needed something else to set himself apart, something besides the obvious way he was set apart from everybody in Marysville, something eccentric that had nothing to do with anything. It wouldn't have been the first time that a person transformed themselves drastically at an early age just to stand out from the crowd. Everybody hides behind something a little bit. Sometimes it's a picket fence, and sometimes it's a billboard.

Most nights at the Badlands Saloon—especially Thursdays, Fridays and Saturday nights—the tables in the middle of the room were occupied by old-timers playing cards. They played early in the evenings, but as the night wore on, the cards were put aside and things usually turned toward random talk and sentimental memories—the good old days—as the drinks began to take hold.

That night Willie Beck was playing some version of gin rummy at the table in the middle of the room with Mildred Zimmerman and Delbert and Mel. Gin rummy is a card game with a specific set of rules, but the games they played late at night at the Badlands Saloon were more organic—the rules weren't set in stone, they were more simple guidelines to keep the games moving along. Oftentimes players would call out variations on the games midway through a hand of cards but nobody really cared, they just went along with whatever had been suggested.

Mildred Zimmerman was an old woman, but that wasn't remarkable—the Badlands Saloon was a place where older people ended up most afternoons and evenings, like a VFW for non-soldiers. Mildred Zimmerman always walked into the bar with great aplomb, wearing a bright magenta feathered boa around her neck, which she wore all year round. She also wore large, Elton John sunglasses with a string of pearls dangling from them so they could hang around her neck when she didn't need them, like a funky old librarian. And she sure didn't need them at midnight on a Saturday night in a dimly lit little bar in the middle of nowhere. But she kept them on.

They impaired her vision, that was plain to see—she bumped into people when she got up to use the bathroom or when she headed to the bar for another drink, scowling that classic old-age scowl of hers—but she kept those sunglasses on anyway, because appearances mean as much to the aged as they do to the young, maybe even more so. Mildred was all made up like she was a television soap-opera star, past her prime, or like she was waiting on a call from the Oscars.

"She looks like she used to be a movie star," I told Mel, nodding over toward Mildred. He laughed. Mel had come over to the bar for another pitcher of beer. He'd been an electrician up at the amphitheater for years and years but now he was retired.

"Boy, you hit that nail right on the head," he said. "She's been wearing that old damned scarf for forty years. And all that makeup and those heels. Christ, look at her—she can hardly walk in those damned old worn-out shoes."

"*Was* she an actress?" I asked him.

"Hell no," Mel said. "She was a donkey in a Christmas play once when we were kids, but that's about it."

Mel was being serious and specific: Apparently Mildred Zimmerman'd filled the back-half of a donkey costume in a Nativity play in 1948. She was just off to the side of the manger, he said, but Mildred couldn't see a thing.

"She's just got a high opinion of herself, that's all," Mel said.

Mildred Zimmerman had never married, Mel told me—she wanted to keep her options open, she'd always say, didn't want to be tied down in case she couldn't shake the acting bug and had to move out to Hollywood. But, of course, she never did move to Hollywood. She'd never left Marysville. She was a clerk at the little bank down the street from the bar, still worked there even though she probably could've retired by then. Maybe she was lonely after all of those years of keeping her options open.

Jimmy Threepence tended to break into old English drinking ballads late at night at the Badlands Saloon and he sounded great to my ears, if a little bit forced. His favorite song—the song he sang nearly every night—was "The Anacreontic Song," a tune from a popular gentlemen's club in London in the 1800s that Francis Scott Key co-opted for "The Star-Spangled Banner." Jimmy Threepence

absolutely loved that song and he sang it out loudly whenever the spirits moved him to sing.

I was sitting there at the bar by myself that night, talking to Kate when she wasn't serving somebody, but mostly just watching everything there in the barroom play out, like an informal Midwestern theater piece. The jukebox was humming along in the background like it always was late at night and there, above all the noise, you'd hear Jimmy Threepence:

> To Anacreon, in heav'n, where he sat in full glee,
> A few sons of harmony sent out a petition,
> That he their inspirer and patron would be;
> When this answer arrived from this jolly old Grecian:
> Voice, fiddle and flute,
> No longer to be mute;
> I'll lend ye my name, and inspire ye to boot;
> And, besides I'll instruct you, like me to intwine,
> The myrtle of Venus with Bacchus's vine.

Jimmy'd be standing there at the end of the bar or out in the middle of the room wailing away, singing very seriously, waving his arms up and down in time with the song. The tables in the room came up to the middle of his chest, and he could only just barely look over the top of the bar when he'd go to order another mug of beer. You'd see him out there, cocked back on his heels, his head thrust back dramatically, hollering out all those old English drinking songs, nobody paying him any attention at all. But by God, that didn't keep him from singing.

Willie Beck bounded over to the bar where I was sitting. "HEH-HEH!" he said, hopping up and down, waving his arms in the air like a fire-child, trying to get Kate's attention behind the bar.

"What's the word, Willie?" I asked him.

"Gin rummy's the word, sonny-boy," he said to me, grabbing my right bicep with both of his hands and shaking me excitedly. "GIN RUMMY!" he hollered out and banged the top of the bar with his fists. He thumped his chest like an orangutan and screamed out above the jukebox and Jimmy Threepence singing there in the middle of the barroom like he was on a stage. Willie Beck was a man full of the spirit. He had an enthusiasm in him that didn't really know any bounds, this sixty- or seventy-year-old man, alive as a firecracker or a newborn baby boy. Some people just have that kind of spark in their bellies.

"How many years have you been coming to this place?" I asked Willie as Kate gave him his beer and a shot of whiskey. I was wearing the hat he'd given me.

"How's that hat fit?" he asked me under his breath, looking at me over the top of his crusty horn-rimmed glasses, his eyes twinkling like Christmas tree lights. "HEH!" He slugged down the shot of whiskey and hollered out again up toward the ceiling like a hyena, slammed the empty shot glass down onto the bar top and snapped his fingers. "I've been comin' in here for a while, young feller." He patted me on the shoulder and wiped the whiskey from his chin with the back of his hand.

"You know, I *have* been comin' in here for a lot of years," he said. "It's somethin' else when you stop to think about it."

Willie stopped twitching and twirling and leaned back against the bar next to me with his mug of beer and looked out across the room. "It's been a long time since I sat down to count the years," he said quietly. Then he slowly raised his head up and let out a massive "WHOOOOOOOOOOOOOP!" He threw his arms up into the air and hopped back over to his card game, past Jimmy Threepence, back into the smoky, never-ending night.

Jazz, Man

The following Thursday morning a man walked into Chains & Whistles, just sort of poking around like all the tourists did, not really interested in renting a bike or taking a tour of the surrounding hills. Most of the people who passed through Marysville had other ideas about how to spend their time on vacation, and sweating out a pedal-bike ride through the Badlands didn't usually fit into those plans.

"Good morning," I said. I was covering Tank's shift so he could tend to a hangover.

"Mornin', sir," he responded with a noticeable drawl. "Got some bicyclin' business goin' on, huh?"

"Yeah, there's some great trails around here," I said. "We could set you up for a ride, if you're interested."

He rubbed his shaggy goatee and shook his head. "Nah, sir, Ah ain't the pedalin' kind." And I suppose that should've been obvious to me when he came in: He was an older, black Southern gentleman, dressed well, but not expensively—semi-shiny loafers, worn khaki trousers and a slightly flashy dress shirt tucked into his pants underneath a rhinestone-inlaid belt.

"Just passing through?" I asked him, nodding toward his faded green pickup truck parked out in front of the shop. It was an older-model truck and it showed its miles. It had a camper built into the truck bed—a sort of John Steinbeck, *Travels with Charley* setup—and a Mississippi license plate on the front bumper.

"Ahm from down south, you know," he said with a little smile. "Ahm on mah way up to Seattle for a recordin' job." It turned out that he was some kind of itinerant Jazz musician—he played the flute—and he was playing and traveling his way out West for a series of low-budget recording dates with a cousin of his who played the Blues in Washington State.

"I'm a big fan of the music," I told him. "Who're you into?"

"Ah, you know, most of 'em. Ahm more of a spiritualist, though, ya know? Ah dig the music in a very deep way."

He was the kind of character I'd have passed right by on the street back in New York City without even noticing, a standard, run-of-the-mill, late-stage hipster. But there in Marysville, way out in the Upper Midwest, he stuck out in a refreshing way. He was maybe sixty or sixty-five years old, but I couldn't be sure. There was something timeless about him, something romantically mystical, a gypsy musician from some other age.

"Ahm Hubert Summerlin," he said, holding out his hand.

"Ollie," I said, shaking his hand. "Ever been to Marysville before?"

"Nah, not really. But Ah been to places like it, you know what Ah mean?" he said, chuckling.

I suppose I did. Hubert started rubbing his chin-whiskers again and looking around, not like he was interested in anything in particular, but more like he wanted to ask me something and was waiting for the right moment to ask it.

"Do you have your flute with you?"

"Yeah, man, got it out in mah pick-'em-up truck."

"You should grab it," I said. "I'd love to hear you play."

"All right. Yeah," he said. "Ah could do that."

While he was rummaging around in the back of his truck for his instrument I set a couple of lawn chairs in front of the cash register and took out my sketchbook. Hubert seemed like a pretty hip cat and I wanted to draw him. Business was slow—there'd only been a trickle of customers all summer long—so it wasn't a problem to sit around and draw when it was quiet if I wanted to.

Hubert came waltzing back into the shop with the little worn black case that held his flute. "Yeah, man, all right," he said and sat down in the lawn chair opposite me, opening the case in his lap and assembling the instrument. It wasn't a shiny flute—it was all tarnished and worn like it'd been around for a while, kind of like his truck.

"How long have you had that?" I asked him, nodding at the instrument.

"Oh man, Ah got this flute when Ah's 'bout yer age, Ah'd think. Yeah, this little girl's been with me for a while now."

He flicked all the keys and they made mute-soft, metallic slapping sounds. He blew into it quickly to get some air flowing and then he started to wail. He started out just noodling around in a low register, to get the thing warmed up, and then he let it out, soaring all over the place, in and out of songs I knew but mostly just blowing free-form, without a care for where it all went. It was incredible hearing those sounds there in that cavernous bike shop. The acoustics were spectacular and I started to draw.

I'd always liked drawing musicians. Back in New York I'd found a bunch of coffee shops and little theaters and bars that had nightly jam sessions. Those kinds of places were perfect for drawing—low lights and handy corners to fade into where nobody paid any attention to me. But musicians don't mind if you look at them while they play anyway—they don't get nervous, they kind of expect you to watch them, I suppose, and I never liked to draw anyone who felt like they were on the spot because it made them nervous and it made me nervous, too. I'd never been much of a performer myself and had always hated the way that drawing in public inevitably turned into a show. Drawing Hubert there at Chains & Whistles that morning was perfect, though, because Hubert Summerlin was a professional. He'd been playing for people for a long time, that much was clear, and he found it easy slipping into himself when he brought his instrument to his lips, just listening and blowing, not too concerned with who or what was happening all around him.

It was part of what had attracted me to Jazz when I was young, that inherent wild abandon that so much of the music is based on. There are a set of rules—a basic framework—but within that framework the world is wide open and anything is possible, very much like drawing or painting: All the basic rules are there—perspective and proportion and lights and darks, basic things like these—but once the pen or brush touch the paper or the canvas, the game is organic and everything is up for grabs, everything is possible, kind of like juggling or like a conversation. You might know what the subject of the conversation is, but that is only the tip of the iceberg. It's all about how the conversation unfolds, how the subject gets described.

"Feels good to play," Hubert told me after five or ten minutes. "You sure Ah ain't gonna get you in trouble here?"

"No, of course not," I told him, looking up from the page. "It's a slow day."

We just went along like that for a couple of hours, Hubert playing and me drawing. He played little riffs from a bunch of standards—"Stella by Starlight," "Take the 'A' Train" (he played that one when I told him I was living in New York City), "Straight No Chaser," "Willow Weep for Me," "On the Sunny Side of the Street," "The Nearness of You"—a ton of great little licks, all played in a solo style. I asked him to play my favorite song—"Stardust"—and he played that one, too. Seasoned Jazz players know all the songs that they should know, and then about a million more on top of that. I did several drawings of Hubert that I really liked and when he asked to see them I showed him the drawings and he liked them, too.

"Where are you staying?"

"Ahm stayin' out north of town a ways at that little campground up there in the park. I got a home on wheels, you know," he said, looking out at his ragged old truck and smiling.

"Are you staying long?"

"Nah, just an evenin'. Ah gotta be out in Seattle by Monday," he said. "You oughtta come out to the campground later. Ah'll trade you somethin' good to eat for one of those drawings in yo book."

"Sounds like a deal," I told him.

He broke down his flute and packed it up. "All right then," he said, "Ah better be gettin' goin'." I told him that I'd swing out after I closed the shop down.

"I might close early this afternoon anyway," I told him. "Nothing's really happening around here today." He walked out and climbed into his pickup truck and fired it up. There was a good amount of smoke coming out of the engine, but it didn't seem to be a problem. Hubert gave me a wave and I waved back.

"Ah'll see ya in a while then!" he hollered and pulled away.

Around five-thirty I shut the lights off there at the shop, slid the massive front door closed and padlocked it. We usually stayed open until sundown, but business was so slow I figured I'd head on out to

where Hubert was staying. Marysville was in the middle of a massive national park—thousands of acres of protected land where herds of buffalo ran wild, mule deer, too, wild turkeys and wild horses. A little two-lane blacktop road curled north out of Marysville into the park, zigging and zagging for thirty or forty miles up into and through the hills and valleys and grasslands and back down into town again—*the Loop*, as everybody called it. At the entrance to the park there was a cattle guard, a staccato of round metal rails spaced four or five inches apart from each other—level with the blacktop road—barbed-wire fences on either side there so the buffalo or the wild horses or the cattle couldn't escape. It's funny what little it takes to keep some things fenced in.

I pushed off from the curb in front of the bike shop and just rolled for a while. The Badlands Saloon was still quiet behind me as I rolled away. I thought maybe I'd pop back down into town after I'd had dinner with Hubert for a drink. Willie Beck would be there then, if he wasn't already.

There was something about getting on a bicycle after a long, lonely day at the bike shop, pushing away from the curb and rolling through that fresh, late-day air. It almost felt like flying, some raw version of freedom that glider pilots must feel, released and let go to sail in absolute silence.

I rode out to the little ticket booth at the entrance to the park, just west of town. There was a per-vehicle admission fee to enter, but as an employee that summer I didn't have to pay—and it was late enough in the day anyway that the park ranger who would normally have been there taking money was already home cooking supper.

It was summertime in Marysville so the sun was still up, but it was working its way down. And that was my favorite time of day in the Badlands, when the shadows started getting long and the colors all around got rich like the raw pigments on a palette. In the evenings, the low-lying areas—before you got up on top of the plateaus—were filled with damp/cool pockets of air, nothing shiver-cold, but more of a refreshing sort of feeling, some kind of reward for having out-lasted the high heat of the day.

The campground that Hubert Summerlin was staying at was called Cottonwood Campground and it was only a mile or so up the blacktop road into the park. I didn't pass a single car in either direction on my way there and when I got to the campground Hubert had the place to himself—just him, a weathered pickup truck and a roaring fire. I coasted down into the campsite on my single-speed bicycle and hopped off, feeling as free and peaceful as a song. "Hey, Hubert. How's supper coming along?"

"Hey, young man. Good to see ya." He was working at the fire pit there beside his truck. I leaned my bike against a cottonwood tree and sat down on the ground next to the fire.

"Care for a beer?" he asked me.

"Yeah, I would," I said.

"It'll calm down here in a few minutes," he said to me, looking at the wild flames of the pit fire he had going. "Ah just gotta get 'er goin'."

Hubert'd changed into a flowing, colorful robe, something close to a bathrobe but more royal and dignified. He had blue jeans on underneath the open robe and sandals on his feet and standing there in the dying June prairie light he almost looked like Moses. *But how does this guy make a living?* I thought to myself.

I was always asking those sorts of practical questions about people I'd meet, especially folks with abstract job descriptions, like Hubert Summerlin: Mystical Traveling Flute Player. *How did he pay the bills?* I tried not to dwell on those mundane, nagging life questions too much, but I certainly considered them from time to time. *Did Hubert Summerlin pay taxes? What about debt? Did Hubert Summerlin have a credit card?* I was always asking myself stupid questions like these. I'd signed up to study how to be an artist at the art school in New York City, but somewhere in the back of my head it all still seemed like a ridiculous notion to me: Making a living selling paintings and drawings. I had a hunch that Hubert Summerlin knew something that I didn't, and I wanted him to tell me about it.

"You've got a pretty comfortable setup out here, don't you?" I said, pointing over at his pickup truck and the picnic table and the fire he was working to control.

"Well, Ah don't require too much to get along, ya know," he said.

He'd strung a bunch of multicolored Christmas lights in two or three lines along one side of his camper and out to a nearby cotton-wood tree, back to the truck and down to an electrical outlet there in the ground. The sun was still up but Cottonwood Campground was down in a little valley so it was getting pretty dim. Hubert had set up some things on the picnic table—Tupperware containers, ceramic cups and bowls, silverware, spices and napkins.

"Thanks for having me over, Hubert," I said as he worked the fire. "What are you cooking?"

"You know 'bout Southern fried chicken, don't ya?" he asked, half looking up at me and half working the fire. Hubert'd stopped by the little butcher shop in Marysville on his way out of town and picked up some chicken legs and wings and a few breasts. "Yeah, man, we'll eat some good stuff tonight," he said with a wink and a smile.

Growing up as I had in Bismarck—highly isolated, on some level, from things that weren't *of Bismarck*—I guess I had never really tasted genuine Southern fried chicken. *Was it a whole lot different from my mom's fried chicken?* I suppose it probably was. Hubert was a Deep-South man and had very likely grown up on fried chicken, the same way folks in New Orleans know about gumbo, or those folks down in the Caribbean know about conch soup.

Hubert fried up the pieces of chicken with several cups of lard in an old cast-iron skillet over the open coals, adding a little bit of salt and pepper every now and then, covering the mix and letting it dance. In a separate pan he fried up some canned baby potatoes with butter, and when it was all ready we sat there on the ground together near the fire and ate. It was dark now and the Christmas lights Hubert'd strung up twinkled there underneath the trees like little stationary fireflies.

"This is delicious, Hubert," I said. "Thank you." The chicken was rich and the canned baby potatoes were a perfect counterbalance. Hubert handed me another beer.

"Yeah, that was a good supper, Ah'd say," he said, taking the napkin from his collar. "Simple and good, man, that's how it oughtta be, you know?"

I did know. Every night back in Bismarck when I was growing up that was the only requirement that my mom made of me and my brother: *Be home for supper at six o'clock.* In a hustle-bustle world, that was an effective ingredient for a strong family. Hubert's supper was down-home Southern fare, but it tasted like *home* to me. It was simple and satisfying, but the meal itself was only an appetizer for the real meal: Conversation. Me and Hubert Summerlin talked and talked throughout the meal about everything from nuclear science to guitar strings (because I played a little bit of guitar, but not in the high Jazz style that Hubert knew so well). We talked about what it was like to be old and what it felt like to be young. We talked about girls and women and where we'd been on both counts. Hubert was something else. He'd been around the block so many times that it made me feel dizzy just hearing about it all—the one-night stands and weddings he'd played, some of the well-known musicians he'd sat in with (he played saxophone with B.B. King's band one night in Indianola, Mississippi). He'd been divorced half a dozen times but he had a new young bride back in Mississippi, a girl barely my age at the time. "I like it that way," he insisted. "I like having a young little somethin' to go home to after a trip like this.

"You got any tail yerself back there in New York?" he asked me.

"Nothing really so far," I said. I'd had my eye on a few girls, but I wasn't a terribly aggressive suitor at that point. Meeting Lacy had certainly tangled me up—she hit me hard on a real gut level, but she was untouchable, and that was probably a big part of it—nobody could ever really *have* Lacy, but the chase was intoxicating. She was a dominant personality, the kind of woman who knew how to take hold of the wheel and drive the car, and that was powerfully attractive to an inhibited young man like myself. I'd been telling myself the usual cliché at that point in my life about how *Art* is a jealous mistress, but I didn't really believe it. I would've traded a painting for Lacy in a second.

Hubert leaned back in satisfaction. He took out a handmade leather pouch and rolled a cigarette. He lit it with a stick from the fire, inhaled deeply and offered it to me.

"Yeah, thanks," I said, taking the crude blunt from him. "You roll your own, huh?" I asked him and smoked. The tobacco was rich and flavorful, something musty about it that I'd never really tasted before. "Is that hazelnut?" I said and started coughing. I was used to smoking cigarettes with filters, I guess. Hubert let out a loud laugh and I handed him back the cigarette. Hubert Summerlin was the picture of ease, there by the campfire.

"Hubert," I said, "are you ever afraid?"

"Whaaat?" he drawled. "Afraid how?"

"Of just living," I said, "just getting by."

"Nah, man," he said and smiled that big old Southern grin of his. "You know, life'll throw everything at ya sometimes, especially when you ain't payin' attention. Ya got to just know that, son. If life can do it to you, it will. That's why I quit worryin' or even thinkin' about it a long, long time ago. Ya know? There's some comfort in that, just acknowledgin' it.

"What the hell you got to be worryin' 'bout anyway? You a young man," he said.

"Well, just the usual basic stuff," I said. "I'm kind of a worrier, I guess. I think about things, like how I'm gonna make a living when I'm finished with school, and who I might marry, and what might kill me." My mind and my mouth were rambling. Hubert passed me the cigarette and I inhaled the smoke again, deeply. "Things like that. You never worry about those things?" I asked him, handing the cigarette back across the open fire. I was getting passionate about it all.

"*Maaaaaaannnnn,*" he said, leaning back, "you got it made in a lot of ways you don't even know. You all right."

Hubert took a long smoky puff on the cigarette and let the smoke rest inside him for half a minute and then blew it out slowly, up into the smoke coming off the pit fire. "There's about a million things in this world that you can get caught up in worryin' 'bout, but don't pay it any mind until you have to. There's a motion to the universe that you can't ever control or even see and there's no use gettin' caught up in *what-ifs* or *maybes.* The whole damned thing plays itself out in spite of what you might think, in a way that you can't never even understand. Just lose yourself in the music of it all, ya know? Transcend it all, get beyond the specifics to the deep-down gut-bottom stuff that you can't never put down on paper.

"I s'pose that's why I play music the way I do, ya know? It's beyond rational, it's all beyond making sense in any sort of logical way. What is *logic,* anyway!" Hubert said emphatically, laughing a little. "There's a rhyme scheme that the universe works by and one that you and me work by, and the two don't have nothin' to do with each other. So all you can do is acknowledge the difference and get on with your business. But always make sure to love a lot," Hubert told me. "Always make sure to love."

I felt then like I understood what Hubert was talking about in a way that I'd never understood anything before in my life. My legs and my arms were tingling, my head was floating and my mind was racing.

"I've never really smoked the hand-rollers much, Hubert," I said, smiling a little sloppily. Hubert looked at me across the embers of the fire. It was pitch-black by then in the campground save for the Christmas lights hanging from Hubert's pickup truck and the trees. Looking up from the colored lights to the starry sky overhead, something struck me as we sat there in silence: All the stars in the sky seemed like variations of the colors of the little Christmas lights down in the campground—blues and greens and violets and yellows and oranges—the Milky Way looked like a speckled rainbow running from one horizon to the other. Occasionally an ember would pop in the fire pit and it sounded like thunder, echoing off the surrounding ancient trees.

"You ain't never smoked, have ya?" Hubert asked me, smiling in the night-light.

"YeahImeanyeahIlikeacigarettejustlikethenextguyespeciallyafter agoodmealcookedoveranopenfireinbeautifulcountrylikethistheway thatthetobaccotastesonafullstomachyouknowIlikethatit'sawonderful digestiveaidyouknowithelpsthefoodandthedrinkandit'salsojustawon-derfulthingsmokingbecauseithitsonallthesensesallatthesametimefeel tastetouchandvisionyouknow?"

Jesus. Did I just say that? I'm talking all out of my head. I feel like I've become instantly retarded, like my brain has been taken out of my head, chewed on by earthworms for a while and then put back in, upside down and back-ward. What's going on? My mind is racing like a devil dog and everything looks kaleidoscopic. Where am I? Am I even here? Irrational questions like these, all racing along inside my head on a current. My body feels electrified and my mind feels like a wet sponge. What if I'm broken? What if I never get any better?

Hubert didn't say anything. He just smiled, sitting there peace-fully across the fire pit from me like a rough-trade Buddha, deep in a secular prayer. The quiet was something else. I'd been living in New York City long enough by then that a silence like that—there at Cottonwood Campground, in the middle of the wilderness—hit me like a beautiful blanket. It was a profoundly meditative feeling, Hubert and me just sitting there thinking our own thoughts in the cool, primitive air of that little valley, the stars all exploding up above

in the sky, up there past the leaves of the cottonwood trees, the air fresh and sharp with a purity that I hadn't really smelled before.

Hubert passed what was left of the cigarette back to me across the fire. I leaned back and took the little sliver to my mouth and smoked and inhaled, holding it in intuitively, as Hubert had, closing my eyes and smiling. All the rational questions I'd been asking Hubert earlier came to my mind, paused there, and then just floated away, up toward Orion. I kept my eyes closed and tasted that rich, musty smoke—I'd never tasted a cigarette like the one Hubert had rolled that night—and there were sounds above me in the trees, but they were sounds beyond me and the trees. It was dark and quiet and I'd never been so comfortable as I was just then, across from Hubert there on the ground, in some sort of timeless reverie.

I opened my eyes, curled up by the fire pit. There was still a warmth coming from the embers, and it was incredibly silent—and black-dark—and I was all alone. Hubert was asleep in his pickup truck camper, but he must've put a blanket over me there by the fire because I was covered up and felt safe and secure. I'd woken up, but I hadn't moved—I'd only opened my eyes, too warm and cozy to move at all—and there in the dead silence I heard very slight rustlings and deep-breathing noises, the sounds of very large lungs breathing in and breathing back out again. I lifted my head up slowly and saw the shadows of a herd of creatures—buffalo—slowly testing the air as they moved through Hubert's campsite, out on some sort of night patrol. I laid my head back down, terrified, but at total peace, too, like it was all just a dream. A casual misstep by one of those multi-tonned beasts would've popped my skull like a grape, but I didn't worry or even think about anything like that at the time. A massive bull buffalo stepped up to me there, lying like a fetus underneath the colorful blanket by the dead fire, lowered his head and sniffed me with a gigantic *SSSSSSSSSSSSSSSSSNIIFFFFF*. He raised up his majestic head and grunted and stepped over me casually, probably thinking to himself *It's just a man!* and passed on with his herd as they moved through Cottonwood Campground.

In the moonlight I watched those massive and ancient creatures of the prairie lumber across the blacktop road that ran through the park, fade a little, and then disappear altogether into the hills.

The Rainbow Connection

I woke up at Wigwam the next morning with a song playing in my head—"The Rainbow Connection"—some kind of cross between Willie Nelson and Kermit the Frog. I'd gotten up just before the sun earlier that morning out at Cottonwood Campground and rode my bike back to the trailer park. I slept like a baby on the couch and felt refreshed in an odd sort of a way, like I'd gone away for a long while in a short space of time and was new again. I showered and threw on some of the same worn clothes I'd been wearing that summer there in Marysville—an old pair of shorts, a homemade sleeveless T-shirt and a pair of sandals—and stepped out the front door of Wigwam. As I closed the door to the trailer I saw a handwritten note hanging there, taped to the outside of the front door so I wouldn't miss it: *"Ollie—See you at the Badlands Saloon tonight? XO Lacy."*

My heart fluttered a little bit. Lacy must've left the note there for me sometime that morning because I hadn't noticed it when I got back from Cottonwood Campground. Maybe Lacy was an early riser? Just the idea of her being there outside the trailer while I was dreaming of buffalo inside Wigwam was about enough to make me skip a beat. There was something about Lacy that made me nuts like a crazy man—she hit me hard in a place that I couldn't control. Lacy was tangible and transcendental all at the same time, but I wasn't in love with Lacy. How could I possibly be? I didn't even know her, and Tank Wilson was my friend. But the feeling was there, right there in the middle of my gut, nothing more complicated than raw lust, I suppose, but it was real real real.

I saddled up my orange single-speed pedal-bike and rolled down

the dirt road that ran through the trailer park. As I passed by Willie Beck's place I saw Willie sitting there on the front steps smoking a pipe. I waved to him as I rolled by.

"Hey-yup," he barked, waving and fidgeting for something in his shirt pocket.

• • •

there goes the new neighbor. new neighbor, new neighbor. i feel like singing this morning. (heh-heh.) never been much of a singer. i like the way it feels, though, to sing. (heh.) can never remember the words to the songs, though. llewelyn's got the t.v. on so goddamned loud in there at the moment. where'd i put that coupon? i got a free sandwich comin' to me at the café today. (heh.) gonna sing and walk and then eat a sandwich. sing and walk and eat a sandwich. it's a hot one out here today. s'pose it should be. that's what happens when it's summertime outside.

• • •

It was a clear, hot afternoon. Willie Beck was just sitting there on his front steps in his worn-out clothes, laughing to himself as I rolled by. Willie reminded me of a lot of things, and I often felt like we were almost related. Although he didn't specifically remind me of any one family member—and God knows my relatives all held personal hygiene in an infinitely higher place than Willie Beck ever did—there was something terribly familiar about him, something almost *familial*. I didn't really know what it was about Willie Beck that made me feel at home. Maybe it was the way he was casually cordial to everybody he'd ever met. Maybe it was because he didn't put too much stock in technology or trends. Maybe it was because his life revolved so closely around friends and family—Llewelyn, as it was, since Llewelyn and Willie were the only family either of them had left. I appreciated that the two of them lived together in that crappy little trailer park trailer late in their lives. Neither of them were bachelor-of-the-month material, but they didn't have to live with each other, either, they each could've lived alone, found an apartment or a small house for themselves in Marysville, some small place that was their own, where they could have some peace and quiet all to themselves. But they didn't. I'd heard Willie complain about Llewelyn a million times that summer, the way that Llewelyn dressed or ate or slept—all the things that Llewelyn wasn't—but they kept on living together anyway, incapable of living alone, or just determined to take care of their family.

Independence Day

The Fourth of July in Marysville was like Christmas Day—all celebration and revelry and hoorahs for 1776 and the birth of the American
dreaming days of our lives. The celebration was unique to the town,
very much a Marysville affair: Around four o'clock in the afternoon
most of the businesses closed down and all the permanent residents
headed home and hung their flags out on their front porches. Then
at five o'clock sharp the city's public address system squeaked and
whined to life and a canned performance of "The Star-Spangled
Banner" thundered and roared and crackled the town to life, all
patriotic and bold and proud, with timpani and crashing cymbals.
The PA system wasn't very hi-tech but the song sounded proud and
majestic anyway. As the song got going Mayor Donald Grinhauser
and his family would leave their house in downtown Marysville with
pomp and purpose, waving and "*Helloing*" the neighbors, marching
down the street following the same old route, carrying little hand-
held flags and sparklers and smiles. Mayor Grinhauser was a pretty
big man—nearly as wide as he was tall—and he had that politician's
way about him, but in a small-town way. He was as genuine as an
elected official could be, but it wasn't a big-time front, because
Marysville was still Marysville and Mayor Donald Grinhauser was, at
the end of the day, still just everybody's neighbor. "Happy Fourth of
July!" he'd holler, romping along in the high summer air.

It was a familiar routine to anybody who'd spent many summers
there in Marysville—as the mayor passed by the houses all the residents would come out and drop in behind him and his family, everybody carrying the same little American flags and sparklers. The parade

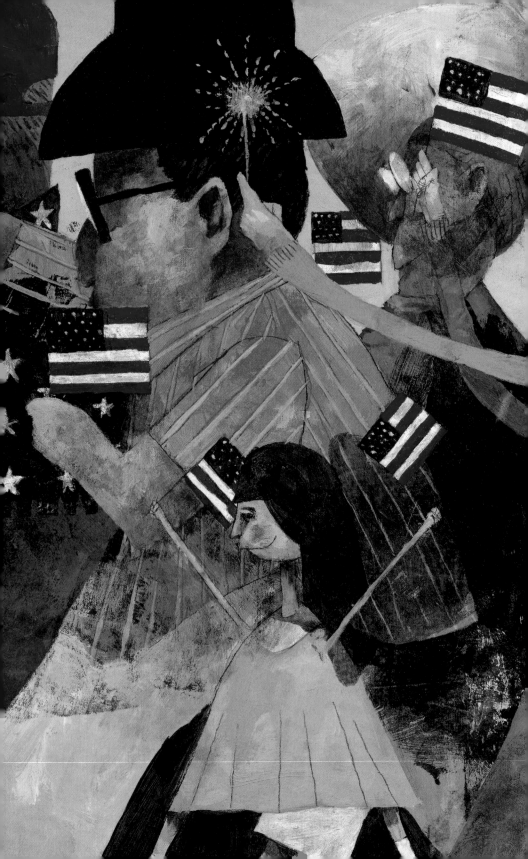

would grow and grow as it worked its way around the little town until every single resident was marching and waving their little flags, laughing and dancing and celebrating. It was something to see, the parade culminating with a big barbecue, live music and square dancing in the little park across the street from Chains & Whistles on Main Street.

I kept the shop open that day even though most of the shops in town had closed down early for the celebration. I set a couple of lawn chairs up out front and just took it all in for a while, the tourists out there in the street and in the park, mingling excitedly with all the locals, like they'd been invited to join an exclusive club or a family for an evening to celebrate and be alive and happy. Everybody was there—Mildred Zimmerman in her flamboyant feather boa, Larry, Mel, Delbert, Big Man and his bookstore wife, though they didn't seem to be talking to each other. And of course Willie Beck, there in the thick of it, drinking beer and dancing. Whenever there was an event like that in Marysville you could count on Willie to be there. He was dancing his side-to-side hop-dance with a bratwurst in one hand and a bottle of beer in the other. He looked happy as hell, like an old man-child without a curfew. There was something about Willie Beck's spirit that was easy to love.

Jimmy Threepence—that crazy-damned-drunken-midget—was there in the middle of it all, too, bellowing out his old English drinking songs. You could hear him a little bit, but just barely—the Country/Swing band that'd been hired from over in Dickinson was really chugging along—a fiddle and a banjo and a guitar and a mandolin and a big upright bass. Some people had started dancing to the music. There were little kids running around and playing games. It was a free-for-all. Kate was there for a second to grab a burger, but she didn't stay long because the Badlands Saloon was still open for business back across the street. And then Lacy rolled by on her skateboard with a cigarette in her long, brown left hand, her black hair floating on the air behind her like a natural cape. She looked like a summertime angel and my heart fluttered a little bit.

"Quite a scene, huh?" Tank had been out back sitting by the creek drinking gin out of a coffee cup and smoking cigarettes. He'd been spending a lot of time doing that, just sitting alone back there by Wallingford Creek, watching the water—even in the afternoons when I'd come in to relieve him he wouldn't leave, he'd just sit out there by himself like he was thinking hard about something, or waiting for something to happen.

"Yeah, it's beautiful," I said. "They do this every summer?"

"Yup. It's like a religion."

Tank sat down in the lawn chair next to me and lit another cigarette. He offered me the packet and I took one. He lit his and then he lit mine and we just sat there quietly for a while smoking our cigarettes. The sun was setting and the streetlights were flickering on. They'd strung a bunch of colorful lamps up across the street, above the barbecues and the band.

"What're you thinking so hard about?" I asked Tank. He was leaning back with his hands behind his head.

"Not a goddamned thing, man," he said.

"You want a burger?"

"Nope," Tank said, wearing his dark sunglasses. "I already ate." He held up his gin-filled coffee cup and smiled.

I got up and walked across the street for a burger or a brat and maybe a beer, too. Willie Beck stopped me on my way.

"Hey-yup!" he said. Willie was still dancing to the acoustic music.

• • •

hey-yup. love to dance, yes . . . sir . . . eee. i'm a dancin' fool! da-dee-da-da. young fella's my neighbor. everybody's here tonight. fun times. llewelyn's home watching t.v. llewelyn doesn't like to dance or barbecue. (heh-heh.) i've always been a dancin' man. even back in school. no girls to dance with, but i still danced-danced-danced. even the slow songs. (heh-heh.) danced with myself. my momma was a good dancer. daddy didn't dance. llewelyn's more like daddy, i guess. who am i like? i'm like myself, i s'pose.

• • •

I was munching through a bag of potato chips and nursing a beer, listening to the sweet summer Swing music when Lacy tapped me on the shoulder.

"Happy Fourth of July," she said and winked and laughed that throaty laugh of hers, looking around the little park across the street from Chains & Whistles.

"Happy Fourth of July yourself," I said. "The bratwursts are good."

The bratwursts are good? Jesus. What a conversationalist! Lacy always tied tied tied up my tongue.

"How's Tank doing?" I asked her, looking back across the street at

Tank Wilson, sleeping in the lawn chair in front of the bike shop. "Seems like he's in a funk."

"Nah," Lacy said. "He's just Tank." She didn't elaborate so I asked her if she'd like a beer.

"Sure," she said. I grabbed a couple of beers from the big, ice-filled tub and we sat on an old wooden fence that ran around the park and listened to the music for a while. It was one of those perfect summer evenings: Cool and still, the darkening sky the color of dark blue steel and just a general feeling of ease in the air, like a celestial "pause" button had been pressed and that evening, anyway, would be *easy*.

We sat there like that for a couple of hours—me and Lacy—drinking beers and taking in the evening. The musical up at the amphitheater was over and everyone was spilling back down into town. The Jigglers showed up and juggled for a while in the street out in front of the Badlands Saloon and it seemed to go over a lot better without the massive fake tits. Everybody loved them at the Independence Day celebration.

"You wanna dance?" Lacy was looking at me that way again with those beautiful dark eyes of hers.

I wasn't a dancer but I liked to dance, sort of like how Willie Beck liked to dance, making it all up as I went along.

Lacy took me by the hand and led me over to where the band was, and the little wooden deck there that was being used as the dance floor that night. The band was playing some Texas Swing—"Waltz Me Across Texas" or something like that in a Bob Wills style—and we just started dancing, simple as that. I'd hold her by her tanned hands, pulling her into me and then letting her drop back to arm's length again, spinning her around occasionally, pulling her into me—her back against my chest—and then spinning her back out again, all in three-four time—um-pah-pah, um-pah-pah—a beautiful late-night, open-air waltz. It was a thrill every time she'd come in close and I could smell her—no perfume, just fresh-aired after a long day of agate hunting at the gravel pits.

We danced and danced like that until the band stopped playing and then we danced one more slow dance, a cappella underneath the colored lights on Main Street in the Badlands. Lacy thanked me and then she just rolled away down the street on her skateboard, back to the Old Hotel.

Standing on the Moon

Hokey Carmichael came into Chains & Whistles to waste some time a couple of weeks after the Fourth of July celebration and I welcomed the company, because riding a bike seemed to be about the last thing on anybody's mind in Marysville. The bumper cars and the Old West Shooting Gallery on the other side of town were making money that summer. The miniature golf course was making money, too. But not Chains & Whistles, and I suppose on some level I didn't really care. Like Tank Wilson always said: *Everything's covered by the Foundation.* Aside from Colonel James Lawrence and his little family, the bike rental business had been slow, slow, slow. Maybe it'd catch on one day, but I didn't see it happening while I was in town.

"What's up," Hokey said, plopping down into one of the lawn chairs I had set up in the shop.

"Coffee?"

"No thanks," he said. He pulled a little silver flask out of his front shirt pocket and took a quick pull. He offered it up to me.

"I'm drinking coffee today," I told him. "You guys have a show tonight?"

"Every goddamned night, brother. It's a brutal schedule and waiting around all day for the show is always the worst part, too. Gotta limit my booze intake," he said and laughed a Woody Woodpecker laugh.

I pulled out a sketchbook and sat down across from Hokey and started to draw him. He had a good face for drawing—serious and clownish at the same time, a little bit weathered for his age, but that only made it more interesting. And like Hubert Summerlin, Hokey was a good model because he was a performer, was used to people inspecting him. He took out his flask and had another healthy little pull of his private whiskey.

"So, seven days a week, all summer long?" I asked him, rhetorically.

"Yeah. It's rough. We're obviously doing it for the money," he said, looking around the shop, smiling.

Apparently the jeering hadn't subsided much, and as the summer had worn on the crowds had gotten more aggressive. The word was out about the Jigglers and some nights now half the crowd—high school kids from over in Dickinson, mostly—were there solely to heckle and hah them. But the Jigglers were professionals. They performed each night like troopers.

"You oughtta come up and see it some night," Hokey told me. "It's quite a scene.

"You want a drink?" he asked me again, offering up his stainless steel portable.

"No thanks," I said.

"What're you doin' tonight?"

"Nothing much," I said, "just drawing and painting out at the trailer, I suppose."

"Why don't you come on up to the amphitheater. I'll meet you at the front gate around seven and get you in."

I finished the drawing and showed it to Hokey and he liked it.

"All right," he said. "I better get going."

I closed the shop that evening and rode out of town on my sleek single-speed orange machine, up toward the amphitheater on top of the hill overlooking Marysville. There was a long, stalled line of cars inching their way up the hill to see the show, carloads of Grandmas and Grandpas and families of out-of-towners, and every fourth or fifth car was full of half-drunk high school students from over in Dickinson, tossing around empty cans of beer and hooting and hollering, high on youth and open-country freedom. I felt bad for Hokey and Hank and Fritz just seeing all those roaring teenage hormones getting unleashed.

Up on top of the hill, the gravel parking lot was filling up fast with people-movers. Fifteen or twenty empty tour buses were lined up there in the setting sun next to the ticket booth. The buses hauled in senior citizens and handicapped people each night for a little fun. North Dakota was an easygoing kind of place, and entertainment like the show there in Marysville each summer was big-time and people came from all over the state for a little taste of that limelight.

"Ollie!" Hokey Carmichael was standing in front of the ticket booth wearing a ratty old bathrobe, waving at me. "Good to see you, man!" Hokey was lit up like a Christmas tree, dripping with bourbon. As the summer wore on, he'd let his guard down a bit when it came to taking the stage sober each night. Maybe the heckling was taking its toll on him.

"Yeah, man, bring your bike with you," he said, waving me over. "Let's go. You can watch the show from backstage."

He led me past the ticket booth and down an *Employees Only* pathway, into the bowels of the theater. Performers were running around everywhere getting ready for the show—half-naked showgirls in their makeup, cowboys and Indians, settlers and sheriffs and gold diggers. The musical up at the amphitheater had a theme each summer, but it didn't vary much—it was an Old Western musical with a handsome young star and a lovely leading lady, but mostly whatever story there was each summer was only a vehicle for the cast to sing songs and dance. There were even live horses and gunfights and an enormous fireworks display at the end of the show each night.

Hokey and I got to the Jigglers' dressing room and I said "Hey" to Fritz and Hank Langhorne who were busy getting their inflatable tits ready. "How's it going, ladies?" I asked them.

"No transvestite jokes, please," Hank said, adjusting his garter belt. "We've heard 'em all."

The Jigglers' dressing room couldn't have been farther from the general feel of the Old Western musical: They had Jimi Hendrix posters taped up to the walls and half a dozen lava lamps spread around the room; they'd taken all the lightbulbs out from around their dressing-room mirrors and replaced them with alternating red and black lightbulbs that gave the room a ghoulish feeling, like you were in a haunted house or a Las Vegas casino.

"How's the bike business?" Fritz asked me while he adjusted his wig. Fritz was wearing a massive black Afro wig, black fishnet stockings and infantry boots. His fingernails were painted black and he was wearing an extremely short, pink miniskirt. *Very sexy.* The whole idea of these guys performing at halftime of the Old Western musical actually started to scare me. It was almost as if they wanted to taunt the crowd, rile them up into some sort of pitched frenzy.

"You guys look great," I said.

Hokey sat down at his dressing-room mirror and started carelessly applying some makeup. He wasn't using mascara brushes or eyeliner pencils—no, he was dipping his bare hands into small jars of colors and smearing them onto his face—a two-fingered streak across his lips for lipstick, a couple of black-blotches on his eyelids—a real Abstract Expressionist approach to the whole process. He turned and looked up at me and slurred: "What'd ya think? Aren't I perdy?" He stood up and twisted an orange, pig-tailed wig onto his head and pointed into the mirror in front of him there in the red-black ambiance of the dressing room: "Honey, you're beautiful," he told his sloppy reflection. I heard explosions and asked Hokey what it was. He produced his stainless steel flask and drank from it passionately. "It's showtime," he said and winked at me.

Hokey Carmichael stumbled out of the dressing room, all dragged-out. There was a little sound booth to the left of the stage where a three-man band manipulated drum machines and soundtracks to back up the singers on the stage. Hokey was buddies with the drummer, and told me to watch the show there with the musicians. "Have fun," he said and quickly left the sound booth. He still had to blow up his tits.

The musical was big and full of fanfare—lots of flags and other patriotic gestures, the kind of stuff that really filled people up with the spirit. All the actors were decked out in big hoop dresses or old-fashioned suits and bow ties and the set changed constantly as the loose story progressed: There was an old covered wagon on the stage and a fake campfire one minute, the next minute a fully formed battlefield with gun smoke and canon fire and military formations. It was all very theatrically realistic, smoke machines and lights and a state-of-the-art sound system. It was really something to see and I was hypnotized for an hour or so.

The crowd clapped enthusiastically as the first half of the show came to an end and the master of ceremonies—a burly old fur trapper—introduced the intermission entertainment: "Ladies and gentlemen, we have a treat for you now. All the way from Los Angeles, California, a colorful group of performers who I know you'll just love. Please give a warm Marysville welcome to . . . THE JIGGLERS!"

Hank Langhorne, Hokey Carmichael and Fritz passed by the sound booth and I waved them on. Fritz and Hank took the stage, but Hokey ducked into the sound booth and pounded me on the shoulder. He looked like a drunk, cross-dressed joker. "HEY MAN YES THIS IS IT!!" he screamed. The musicians looked at each other and laughed like they'd seen it all before. "This is showbidness," Hokey Carmichael whispered to me. He had his flask with him and he took a long pull on it until it was empty. I could see Fritz and Hank Langhorne out on the stage through the window of the sound booth, taking in only a smattering of applause.

"Here . . . Thisisforyou." Hokey handed me the empty stainless steel flask and whipped out of the sound booth and onto the stage. It was amazing that he could even walk, but he bounded out there like a cougar in the spotlight. The drummer in the sound booth crashed a gong.

"Hello, ladies, and especially you gentlemen!" Hank lisped and started to juggle some custom-made, multicolored clubs. I thought that maybe the Jigglers were taking this whole androgynous thing a little too far—they were really hamming it up, curtsying around the stage on their tippy toes while they juggled in a triangle formation, the rainbow juggling clubs flying back and forth between them like a shaky kaleidoscope. They were all miked-up and they bantered with each other while they juggled: "Fritz, you look beautiful tonight." "Hokey, your eyeliner is bleeding." "Screw you, Hank. This is art." That's what Hokey Carmichael said. He could barely stand up, but he managed to juggle with the other two—nine clubs between the three of them—whipping and flailing the things back and forth, back and forth, over and over again, no music or soundtrack, just the catch-slaps and whoosh-throw sounds of the juggling clubs being passed around. At first the booing was intermittent, a lone catcall here and there from the Badlands amphitheater audience. But as the Jigglers worked their way through their routine, the hollers and bad talk crescendoed, drowning out the Jigglers' banter and generally overwhelming the whole performance.

They put away their customized juggling clubs and Hokey went to the back of the stage where their kit box was sitting and pulled out a chain saw. He fired it up back there in the shadows and hit the trigger three times fast—*VROOM-VROOM-VRRRRROOOOOM!* Smoke from the saw flooded the stage. Hokey spun around on a flip-flop heel and fell over with a mute *thud,* down onto the stage. He leapt up fast, though, and ran out to the edge of the stage and gunned his rig again—*VROOM-VROOM-VROOM-VROOM-VRRRRROOOOOM!*

This was Hokey Carmichael's portion of the performance. Hank and Fritz happily left the stage and Hokey set his smoking chain saw down—still rumbling—and stood there taunting the audience for almost an entire minute, which feels like an hour in show-business time. He went back to the kit box at the back of the stage and grabbed two more chain saws, one in each hand. He fired those monsters up, too, and marched back out to the front of the stage—up there above the audience—and started to juggle the damned things, all three of them roaring and screaming. Sitting in the sound booth at the side of the stage, I couldn't believe my eyes. *How the hell did he get those things airborne and how long could he maintain it all?* He was staggering under the weight of the chain saws, hobbling back and forth—dropping down to one knee occasionally—barely alive up there in the harsh lights of the amphitheater, bobbing and weaving like an underdog prize fighter, the boos pounding down from the audience almost as loudly as Hokey Carmichael's industrial arts chorus. His massive inflatable tits were a burden, too, wobbling around there underneath his green bikini top like a couple of over-sized cantaloupes.

Hokey barely finished his routine up at the amphitheater that night. The boos had turned into waves of disapproval by the time he'd put the chain saws away, so Hokey just curtsied, winked at the audience and smiled. Fritz and Hank joined him back onstage and they carried on with their nightly show. From what I could see from inside the sound booth the stage looked like a matte-gray half-moon, a lonely place that I never cared to visit. But the Jigglers carried on, juggling all sorts of things—throw pillows and apples and oranges and marbles, eggs and rings and beach balls—and the boos just grew and grew and grew. The Jigglers were talented as hell, but the whole thing was just too much to watch, that battle out there between off-the-wall performance art and the lynch-mob mentality of the crowd.

I slipped out of the sound booth, grabbed my bike back in the dressing room and headed back down into Marysville, the sounds of a riot trailing off behind me as I rolled away.

Rainy Days, Wet Trails

132   The next day it rained. It was dark clouds all morning, the water dropping out of the sky hard and heavy, turning the dirt road that ran through the trailer park there west of Marysville into a little muddy river. Wallingford Creek crested around midday and half the campground had to be evacuated by the park rangers.

But I'd always liked rainy days, that cozy isolated womb feeling, like a sick day when you were a kid in school, only better, because everybody was in the same boat on a rainy day. Making paintings and drawings is like a perpetual rainy day, on some level, because making paintings and drawings is a lonely business. It *has* to be a lonely business. Art isn't a team sport—it's not made by committee—it's just you you you there in front of the paper or the canvas, trying to give some kind of form to all those formless things in the world and in your wild mind. It's a contradiction, really, making drawings and paintings—the act itself almost *emphasizes* your aloneness, because there's only enough room in front of that blank page for one person and that one person has to be *you*. In the making of the thing, though, you're inherently connected with the rest of the world around you, trying to freeze it all—time capsule it—and in that you can never really be alone.

There wasn't a phone at Wigwam so there was nobody to call, but it didn't look like there'd be anything much going on in town that day so I just stayed home, drinking coffee, drawing and painting.

• • •

rain, rain, go away, come again some other day. (heh-heh.) no. don't go away, rain. i like the rain. always have. don't like the blizzards so much, though. llewelyn always sleeps when it rains. he's sleepin' down the hall right now. snores, too, loud as hell. i can see the lights on over there in the young feller's trailer. young feller's a nice kid. just passin' through. it seems like everybody's always just passin' through. everybody's on their way to someplace else. i've never really been anywhere. where the hell would i go? france? nope. (heh.) i never wanted to go anywhere and i never wanted to wear a beret. i always liked it right here where i've always been. i think i'm almost outta tobacco. smoke the pipe in the daytime and smoke cigarettes all night long. (heh-heh.) i wonder when the young feller's gonna leave? he's been a good neighbor. never comes and bothers us. (heh-heh.) i can't ever figure out if i like to be bothered or not. i s'pose everybody likes to be bothered sometimes. except for llewelyn. nobody ever bothers him. he sleeps a lot. i sleep pretty regular. got too much energy, though. i think too much sometimes and can't sleep. sometimes i just lay awake thinkin' 'bout all the things i didn't do. maybe i'll go back to school. (heh-heh.) barely made it out of high school the first time around. (heh.) maybe i'll go back, though, and be a doctor. no—not a doctor—i'll be a veterinarian. yeah. no. not a veterinarian. i'll go back to school and study on how to be a horse or a dog. (heh-heh.) yeah. i'll go back to school and learn how not to talk to myself or think so much. (heh.)

Wigwam was really taking on the air of a well-worn art studio. You could see it there that afternoon—paintings and drawings tacked up to all the walls of the trailer—pictures of Willie and Tank and Lacy and Chains & Whistles, all the people and things I'd seen and known there that summer, a few landscapes of the Badlands around Marysville, all the rich colors in those hills, the reds and umbers and greens. Sometimes I'd just sit down on the couch with a cup of black coffee and look at all those drawings and paintings and think about it all. It was like looking back on a time that was still taking shape—past, present and maybe even some kind of future—a colorful fourth dimension outside of linear time. Paintings and drawings can do that to you, they can take you to places in your mind that don't exist or even make sense, but a lot of the time those places are more tangible and real than anything else you could ever really know.

I stood up and walked over to the front door and the little window there and looked out across the yard through the pouring rain at Willie Beck's trailer. There was a light on in one of the windows

and through the rain I could see his silhouette—Willie Beck—sitting there in his trailer smoking his pipe and talking to himself. The shadow bopped back and forth—an occasional flash from a lighter and then darkness again—and for a second, through the rainy Marysville trailer park afternoon, I thought I could see Willie Beck laughing.

136

Night Moves

The high heat of the summer was on top of Marysville. The evenings were still pretty hot—even after the sun had gone down—and the heat that lingered after dark did something to the Badlands Saloon. The barroom was a little stuffier at that point in the summer, the air was a little bit heavier—heavier than back in June—but it wasn't uncomfortable. It was a *comfort*, in fact, that warm/hot feeling of the Badlands Saloon at the height of the summer, the same way I'm sure it was a hell of a good place to be in the middle of February, when everything outside was frozen stiff and nobody went outside unless they had to.

It was Saturday night again and things were really swinging. The Badlands Saloon was packed with most of the regulars, cigarette smoke hanging around the ceiling like mountain mist. Lacy was drinking for free like she always did, Larry was cracking jokes and Mel—the retired electrician and resident armchair philosopher— was talking about Kierkegaard, Kant and Descartes, but not necessarily in that order. And me, I was just taking it all in—the music, the mood, the moment—my hands grease-stained from the bikes, my legs a little bit tired from the solo rides outside of town. Behind the bar Kate looked like Fred Astaire, dancing out some highly choreographed routine.

There was a flash of movement in one of the windows at the front of the bar. I caught a glimpse of it and turned to look—a flash of red flashed again outside the screen door, then another streak of color and light in the other window at the front of the bar and then a quiet *thud* mixed in with the jukebox music and the other various

loud chitter-chatters coming from the barroom. I think I was the only one who noticed the action out front. Everybody else was lost in their own private worlds. The door to the bar whipped open with a crack and a little man in a red hooded sweatshirt nearly fell into the bar, caught himself, squinted, closed his eyes again and started stumbling toward me. I was standing at a raised table opposite the front door, back near the pool table with Larry and Willie Beck. This blurry phantom staggered through the crowded room straight over to our table, like we'd somehow planned it all out. But we hadn't planned anything. This scrawny-looking man-child came right up to where we were drinking and talking and stopped.

"Hey," I said as he wobbled to a stop next to me. He didn't really answer, just rocked back and forth, half looking at me and half not. He was a Saturday-night reincarnation of those inflatable children's punching bags, the kind that are weighted down at the bottom so when you punch them they bob backward toward the floor and then bob back up again, ready for more. The other people at our table had noticed the dark visitor standing there swaying next to me and stopped talking. The smiles of casual conversation slipped from their faces and we all stood there for a second, staring at this *thing* that had joined our party, a real-life cross between Golem and Rumpelstiltskin.

"Hey, man, who are you?" Larry asked. Larry was the guy at the bar who knew everybody, or got to know everybody. He had no trouble at all starting up a conversation. The little man in the red hooded sweatshirt straightened up and tried to open his eyes, the way serious drunks will, imitating a kind of dignified sobriety. He pulled up the left sleeve of his sweatshirt and pointed a bony finger at the sloppy blue moniker tattooed there on his bicep:

"Smoochie!" he slurred, quietly. He looked up at us with a furrowed brow and screamed, *"SMOOOOOCHIE!!"* There we were. Introduced.

"Nice to meet you, Smoochie," Larry said.

Normally, when a guy looking like Smoochie did that night—in his ragged-wild condition—comes into an out-of-the-way bar well after midnight, it'll make you a little nervous. But Smoochie, as he was—beyond drunk, so drunk it hurt your head just to look at him— wasn't a threat to anybody. He was a long ways from putting two and two together. He wasn't even a threat to himself at that point, the way toddlers are indestructible—they fall and don't really hurt themselves because everything is limp, their bodies are at some sort of natural truce with gravity. That's where Smoochie was at.

"Where ya been, Smoochie?" Larry asked him, not really intending for the question to be taken seriously, but more as a half-joke at Smoochie's expense, which clearly wasn't the first one Smoochie'd ever suffered.

"Ah jus gotouttah jail!" Smoochie blurted out. "Been there for twenny-five years. July seveenth, nineneen-seveneetwo." His answer to Larry's question was too specific and Smoochie was too far gone for it to have been a lie. The math certainly worked out, and Smoochie's face and withered little body backed it up. He was still a fairly young man—early forties, maybe—but he looked a lot older. I suppose prison does that to a man—time marches on outside the walls but the body's sort of frozen at the age you're at when you go in. From a distance, Smoochie still looked like the nineteen- or twenty-year-old young man who'd made a mistake, but up close he was unnaturally weathered, beaten down by an institutionalized aging.

"Jesus, Smoochie. What'd'ya do to be in the clink for so long?" We were all wondering the same thing, but Larry was the kind of guy to ask a question like that. Smoochie leaned back on an unsteady leg, raised his right hand, stuck out a forefinger and cocked his thumb to look like a pistol:

"I shotaman," he said emphatically with a sigh, and then closed his eyes again and staggered a little bit. Larry asked Kate for another mug and poured a glass of beer from the pitcher we were all sharing.

"Here ya go, Smooch," Larry said, handing Smoochie the sudsy mug. "Drink up."

I'd moved over to the bar by myself. Over at the table Larry and Willie had fallen back into their evening and Smoochie was just standing there, slowly rocking back and forth, part of the gang, as it were, but all alone, too.

Kate looked at me from behind the bar, raising her eyebrows and nodding toward my empty glass, the universal inquiry: *"Another one?"* I smiled and nodded, handing her my glass. I turned back toward the barroom and just watched it all. Nothing ever really changed at the Badlands Saloon, late on a Saturday night—everybody was there and most everybody who was there had been for a hundred Saturday nights in a row, more or less, so they certainly weren't coming back over and over again to find something, to discover something that they couldn't find outside the doors of that bar. And that was the point, I guess: They all just wanted someplace where they could lose themselves for a little while, to be someplace where they didn't have to ask any questions.

Kate handed me a whiskey and I paid her. She always seemed to accept the money reluctantly. I leaned against the bar and sipped the icy amber. Lacy was lingering around down by my end of the bar, near the pool table, a sort of free-wheeling goddess, dark and native and forbidden—untouchable, somehow, and not necessarily because she was Tank Wilson's girlfriend. It had something more to do with my knowing then that Lacy knew a whole hell of a lot more about *The Dance* than I would know for a long time. But I loved her for being a woman, her long brown arms and her general easy-drinking ways. She was the kind of girl you'd never bring home to Momma. She was the kind of girl you'd never bring home to anyone because you'd just as soon have her all to yourself, in secret, where you could love her like you'd always wanted to love a woman, completely and wholeheartedly without a strain of holdback. Lacy brought that out in me—she brought it out in everybody who ever met her at the Badlands Saloon, or at the quarry or at the gas station where they sold her agate key chains. Lacy was freedom to the eyes of the world. Lacy wasn't an Indian girl or a skateboarder or a drinker or a thinker or a high school dropout. Lacy just *was*. She was her own pattern, unquestionably alive and undeniably beautiful without even trying. And she knew it. Everybody knew it.

Lacy and Tank had been dating on and off for a few years by the time I got to Marysville. Or at least they sought refuge in each other's company each spring when Tank would come back to Marysville from Bismarck, where he had some other sort of seasonal job during the winters. I don't know if they were ever truly in love, the way that lovers are. I don't know if either of them was capable of that kind of love. They were both just too free in their spirits. In that, though, their being together made sense. But it had been slowly falling apart after my arriving in Marysville, and later that summer it was all sunk, as far as the two of them were concerned. Tank was drinking hard and he was getting sloppy—loose and untethered, lacking the daily focus that life and love require. More and more often, when he'd come into the Badlands Saloon late at night when things were rolling along, Lacy would barely acknowledge him, and on some level I don't think Tank really even cared.

Lacy'd seen me standing there at the bar all by myself. She gave me one of her smiles and walked over to where I was standing. There was an empty stool there at the bar, so I pulled it out and offered it to her. She winked and sat down and crossed her legs. "Quite a night," I said, taking a long courage drink of whiskey. Lacy lowered her head and zeroed in on my eyes with hers and smiled again. I laughed. "Are you winning over there?" I asked her, nodding back toward the pool table. Lacy smiled and nodded back at me. I was going a little bit crazy by then that summer, because Lacy had made it abundantly clear that there was something about me that she wanted to touch. We were playing a game, where she was pushing ferociously—subtly—toward something that she knew wasn't a given with me. Part of it might have been simple loyalty to Tank, on my part, but it was more than that, too, and Lacy knew it damned well because she'd been playing the game a lot longer than I had. I was innocent in almost every way—I was a little bit afraid of being a main character in the game of life, I suppose, and maybe that was why I made drawings and paintings, because painting and drawing were a way to get at the world without really being a part of it, a way to live without having to risk life's consequences. *Was Art a cop-out?* I'd considered that question more than a couple of times, but I never really believed it. *Is life a reflection of Art? Is Art a reflection of life?* These were stupid art school questions, I figured, and they didn't mean anything. Drawing and painting were as much a part of life for me as taste and touch.

"T. B. Sheets" came up on the jukebox. "KAAAAATTTEE!!" I hollered and pointed toward the volume knob there on the wall behind the bar. Kate smiled—mid-stride, like she always was good enough to do—and cranked the song up:

> *If you wanna hear a few tunes, I'll turn on the radio for you.*
> *There you go, there you go, there you go, baby, there you go . . .*

I worked up all the energy in my world: "LACY!!!" I screamed over Van Morrison blaring on the jukebox, "CAN I BUY YOU A DRINK!?"

"Okay," she whispered. "Gin-tonic," she said, and it was almost like nobody else in the place could have heard her there under her breath except me, and I suppose it was true. She smiled at me and I felt a wild savage lust I'd never felt before, had never felt quite so real, that feeling then, just within reaching distance.

Kate handed me Lacy's gin-and-tonic across the bar. I couldn't remember if I'd even officially ordered the thing. Kate probably just read the situation for what it was.

Lacy was holding her pool cue in one hand—a house cue—and took the gin-and-tonic with her other hand, beautiful long brown fingers, forever naturally tan. She raised the glass a little bit, toasting me, nodded and smiled and took a long sip with those lips of hers. True pool players know that house cues are for shit—all crooked and overused—but it made perfect sense for Lacy to be playing with one because she could beat anybody with a house cue. Lacy could beat you with a bamboo pole blindfolded, if she wanted to. The Badlands Saloon wasn't a pool shark hangout, but by God she knew she could play and she worked it to her advantage expertly, drinking as much as she ever cared to without ever reaching for her wallet. A girl like Lacy could drink for free anyway, because she was beautiful and witty, but I think she preferred to earn hers.

"Thanks for the drink," she said, winking. She looked at the faded pictures behind the bar on the wall there, and then at me in the reflection in the mirror behind the bar. She stroked my leg with her pool cue, just barely, then she looked at me for real—not in the reflection behind the bar, but over at me, straight into my eyes. I turned and looked at her. Tank was down at the other end of the bar, slumped over into himself, asleep and oblivious. I looked at Lacy again and she stared into my blue eyes with her big brown ones and smiled that incredibly all-encompassing smile of hers, a smile so big that it crowded out just about everything else in the bar-room, all the noise and the smoke and the smells, they all just disappeared. I had to look away and catch my breath.

"Do you wanna go for a walk?" she asked me.

"Yeah, okay."

• • •

Lacy and I stepped out onto the street there in front of the Badlands Saloon and we just started walking. The music and the chatter from back inside the barroom lingered with us for a while, but by the end of the block it was pretty much just quiet, only the crickets and the stars. Lacy was still carrying her pool cue.

"Are we going to play some pool?" I asked her. Lacy smiled and kept on walking, using the cue like somebody with a cane who didn't really need one, sort of tapping the street as we went along. She reached into her front blue jeans pocket and pulled out a pack of American Spirit cigarettes, took one for herself effortlessly and then flicked one to the fore of the hard-pack for me. She offered it to me without a word. I took the cigarette, walking along beside her. She lit her own cigarette, and then she lit mine with an eternal Badlands flame.

"What's your story, Ollie?" she asked me. We were heading east down the middle of Main Street, past the historic Old Hotel where Lacy lived and on toward the edge of town, which wasn't a very long ways to go in Marysville. I laughed. Lacy was as intimidating as hell in the daytime, but now—just walking along there like a couple of troubadours—I didn't think about anything much at all.

"What do you want to know, Lacy?" I asked her, blowing smoke up toward the stars.

"Nothing, really." She looked over at me there underneath the last streetlamp on the east side of town, then she smiled, smoked on her cigarette and we kept on walking.

There were two churches in Marysville, one Catholic and one Protestant. Lacy and I were standing in front of the Lutheran church—Trinity Lutheran Church. We climbed up the steps of the church and sat down in front of that holy house like a couple of Sunday school children. "We should probably take our shoes off," I said, removing one sandal and then the other one. Lacy smiled and took off her canvas high-top sneakers.

After a while we stood up and moved off into the shadows along the side of the church, onto the damp, dewy grass, over to a little swinging love seat next to a birdbath where I'm sure the pastor liked to sit and watch the sunsets. "What's *your* story, Lacy," I asked her, sitting down in the swinging chair. Lacy leaned her pool cue against the far side of the swing and sat down next to me. The contraption moved a little, so I pushed against the wet grass underneath our feet and we started slowly rocking—back and forth, back and forth—little squeaks in the silent night.

"I got no story," Lacy said, and I was sure she smiled her smile up at me in the darkness.

"You've got a story," I said. "Maybe it's just a complicated one."

"Nah, it's a pretty simple one, really." Lacy rested her head on my shoulder and her hand on my thigh. I was wearing shorts so her hand was on my thigh flesh, firm and real, and it made me quiver underneath all the whiskey and the beer.

"You're a beautiful woman, Lacy," I said quietly. I felt like I was in the middle of a dime-store romance novel, but nothing had anything to do with romance or love or courtship. This was all simply visceral, very much present tense.

Lacy reached over with her left hand and grabbed me by the ear and pulled me down toward her and kissed me on the mouth, as long and hard as I'd ever been kissed before. She sucked on my lips and slowly flashed my mouth with her tongue. I was an inexperienced youngster, but she kissed me with a force that had to have been unique. It was like she couldn't wait any longer, and her not waiting disarmed me, too, and I kissed her back hard with a ferocity and an urgency that was pure wild abandon.

Lacy's pool cue fell against the stones beneath our rocking chair with a cracking sound, but we didn't stop. The chains holding the rickety old swinging chair squeaked very softly in the Marysville night. The only other thing I could hear was the way Lacy felt in my hands—all the inexperienced voices in my head had been put on notice, or had been banished altogether.

I took off Lacy's T-shirt and threw it on the ground. It landed there on top of her pool cue, next to the rosebush and the birdbath. She slipped my shirt over my head and straddled my lap in a single motion. She was a tangible shadow on top of me there in the darkness, and when she leaned down to kiss me again her long black hair drowned out the entire world and I felt like I was standing all alone on the surface of the moon, staring back at the Earth with that wicked rush of vertigo bubbling in my stomach.

I stood up, holding Lacy in my lap, clenching her soft thighs. I carried her over to a weeping willow tree at the rear of the church building and we crawled underneath the drooping, fragrant branches there and undressed on the freshly cut grass. Neither of us could see a thing save for what we could feel, and there were more colors in what Lacy and I were feeling on that velveteen night than in any rainbow that ever graced a Badlands summer sky. No words were spoken and when we were finished we just laid on the cool grass panting, huddled together, sweating like deer hiding from hunters. It was a peaceful stillness in Marysville and we fell asleep together, but neither of us dreamed. Our minds were at ease.

Solitaire

By the time I got to Chains & Whistles the next afternoon Tank Wilson was already tanked, slouched down in a lawn chair behind the cash register toward the back of the shop, his dark sunglasses just visible above the counter. "Wass-up," he slurred out when I pulled in. He was thumbing through a deck of playing cards that he kept around the shop for games of solitaire on rainy days. It was a sunny day in Marysville.

"Long night, shorty?"

That was a strange question. *Did Tank know?* I shrugged the whole thing off and parked my bike in one of the racks at the far side of the shop.

"Anybody sign up for a ride this afternoon?" I asked him. He pulled a black queen from the deck of cards.

"No sirree," he said. "It's 'nother bust, Ollie-boy."

The previous night was a dream to me when I finally woke up on the couch out at Wigwam, but I could remember every detail, clear as a picture: Lacy's lips and her cool smile, the smell of the damp grass there in the dark churchyard, the way Lacy tasted and smelled, all of her—wild and smoky and tangy—not a store-bought taste, but something fundamentally natural, real and pure. What me and Lacy had done couldn't have been a sin. It wasn't a poison apple served up by some serpent in the midnight grounds of Marysville's only Lutheran church. *Right?* Yes. Right. No sins had been committed that night. I'd never been much of a Casanova and Lacy was a wild and free spirit with her own set of rules that she carried with her wherever she went. There was nothing rational about any of it.

Tank tossed the deck of cards onto the counter next to the cash register and stood up with a long sigh.

"Ahhhhhhh yeah," he said. "It's that time of the summer."

I sat down in a lawn chair on the other side of the cash register—the same place where I'd drawn Hubert Summerlin and Hokey Carmichael earlier that summer—took out a sketchbook and a reliable pen.

"I think I've about had it with this place," Tank continued. He put his hands in his pant pockets and walked around slowly in irregular circles, aimlessly around the work area in the back of the shop. "Do you like this place?" he asked me, pausing for a second. It was a rhetorical question: *Did I like this place?* There was something about the way Tank just lobbed that question out into the air, not really expecting an answer. It was a big question and I wasn't sure how to answer it, so I just started drawing Tank Wilson and he went on:

"I tell ya, man, I don't know if I like it here anymore. It's an easy job, but everything here is starting to feel a little bit *empty*. D'ya know what I mean? What's the point, anyway? What the hell am I doing out here in the middle of nowhere? Marysville," he said with a half-laugh, looking down at the concrete floor. "Where the hell is Marysville? It's feeling more and more to me like Marysville is *nowhere*."

Tank Wilson took a bottle of Kentucky bourbon from underneath the counter and set it down next to the cash register. "You know, it's not even Marysville. I've always had this feeling that wherever I am is broken—not broken in any sort of real sense, but broken in a subtle kind of way, like the machinery just ain't workin'. D'ya know what I mean?" I drew Tank Wilson's hat and part of his face, his sunglasses and his strong jaw. "Like the teeth on the cogs of the machine are all worn down like an old man's teeth or somethin'," he said. "It's all just a weird, lonely feeling."

Tank unscrewed the cap on the bottle of whiskey with his gnarled bike-shop hand and filled up his coffee cup two-thirds of the way and put the bottle away, back underneath the counter. There was some lukewarm coffee in a thermos and he put some of that into his mug of whiskey, too, sipped it and sighed again.

"I don't know. Maybe it's just life. I always wonder if things could be different, like if I started all over again somewhere else, in Los

Angeles or Santa Fe or Toronto. Someplace like that. Maybe I should just leave the country altogether." Tank Wilson laughed a half-hearted laugh again and drank from his ceramic cup.

As I drew Tank Wilson at Chains & Whistles that afternoon, I understood what he was saying: *Sometimes life is tedious and hard—terrifying—where three-quarters of the time none of us has got any real clue as to why the hell we're doing what we're doing in the first place.* I figured the first thing to do was not to think about it too much.

Tank went on: "I mean, how has New York been treatin' you? It must be a whole helluva lot better than this place." Tank threw his arms out, spilling half of his whiskey-coffee onto the greasy shop floor. "I'd like to go to New York City someday," he said. "I'd like to go anywhere someday."

Drawing Tank there that afternoon, it was almost as if I wasn't there at all, like I was witnessing some sort of interior monologue on an off-Broadway stage, a rhetorical dialogue between Tank Wilson and himself. But I *was* listening closely to what he was saying that afternoon, everything he was saying and all the things that he wasn't saying, too. My mind was going a thousand-miles-an-hour by then that summer with all the same old thoughts and anxieties, but none of it had anything to do with *where* I was. Marysville was an out-of-the-way place, sure, but the thrills and fears of just *living* know no borders, they follow you around like an animated shadow, pulling and tugging at you, sometimes even lifting you up toward heaven.

Tank Wilson walked out behind the shop and lit a cigarette there alongside Wallingford Creek. I closed my sketchbook, got up and walked to the front of the shop and stood there in the massive front doorway with a cup of coffee, watching the tourists stroll by or zoom past on motorcycles, saying "Hey" occasionally, but not even bothering to try and sell any of them on a bike rental. People came to Marysville in the summertime for all sorts of different reasons, but riding a bike sure wasn't one of them.

Bingo

The August days flew by in Marysville. They seemed like forever-days at the time, like youth-days will, but they were disappearing. I was sitting at the Badlands Saloon when Tank Wilson came stumbling in, looking a lot like Smoochie had earlier that summer—real rough, like his gyroscope was broken. "HEYYIUUAAADOIN'?" he throbbed, wobbling a stool up to the bar. He didn't look at anybody and he didn't look too good. It was an early-evening Wednesday at the Badlands Saloon and it was Bingo Night, a weekly hump-day ritual where Kate would turn the crank on the old iron cage and pull out Ping-Pong balls with the letters on them—"B," "I," "N," "G" or "O." It was an old, slow game, but Marysville was that kind of a town, and the Badlands Saloon was that kind of a place.

Tank had insisted that I close the shop down early that afternoon, something about him having things to do and how he didn't want the bike-rental business hanging over his head. Nothing was going on at Chains & Whistles anyway and I was feeling more and more like a mannequin in a storefront window by then that summer, hardly a mountain bike tour guide. So I'd taken my bike out for a quick spin up into the hills south of town where the views never ended and never got old, and then back down into town, to the Badlands Saloon and Bingo Night.

"We'llplaybingookay?" Tank Wilson had his dark sunglasses on—he wore them all the time by then that summer—but I could still tell that his eyes were nearly shut. He told me we'd play bingo not so much as a statement or a question, but almost pleadingly, like a game of bingo was a life raft that afternoon, something to hang on to for a couple of hours.

"Yes, Tank," I said, "we'll play some bingo."

The jukebox was playing soft Country music and Kate was setting the game up, the rickety iron cage with the lettered Ping-Pong balls, the stack of bingo cards and the little cardboard squares to cover the called letters. Jimmy Threepence came waddling into the bar whistling an old English drinking song, smoking a cigarette. Mildred Zimmerman was there, too, wearing her bright magenta feather boa, sitting at a table with Mel and Delbert and Larry, all of them drinking beer. Kate came down the bar to where me and Tank were sitting.

"Hi, Ollie. What can I get ya?"

"A beer please, Kate," I said.

Kate bent down to the cooler behind the bar to fetch my beer and Tank blurted out: "AH'LLHAVEAWHISKEYPLEASEKATETHANK-YOU!" Kate paused for a moment, giving Tank a half-smile. She was always so understanding.

The front door of the barroom opened and Lacy came walking in with her skateboard under her arm. The streetlamps had started glowing outside as the sun went down on Main Street. Lacy was a dark silhouette in slow motion for a second as she passed behind me and Tank sitting at the bar. "Afternoon, gentlemen," she said nonchalantly without breaking her stride, walking over to a table in the middle of the barroom and sitting herself down next to Larry. She had such an easygoing way about her. My heart started racing just seeing her again, but she was as casual as the breeze.

The front door of the bar opened again and Willie Beck came waltzing into the room, clapping his hands and doing a slow little jig. He came over to me at the bar and thumped me on the shoulder a couple of times and said: "Bingo-time, eh young feller?"

"Hey, Willie, how're you doing?" I asked him, but Willie was already hopping down the bar to corral Kate for a drink.

"Hi, Willie," she said. "A beer?"

"Hey-yup," he said and spun around once pretty gracefully on his worn-out shoe heel. There was Willie Beck, I thought—smack in the middle of everything, singing his own special song and dancing his own special dance.

• • •

bingo bingo bingo! must be wednesday if we're all playin' bingo. (heh.) every-
body's here. not everybody, but i recognize everybody here. so for now, i guess
this is everybody. (heh-heh!) wonder if i'll win at the bingo today. winnin's
hard. all those ping-pongers spinnin' 'round and 'round and 'round, all
mixed up. you never know, you never know, you never know. (heh.) but
maybe it's my lucky day.

•   •   •

Kate killed the jukebox and handed out the bingo cards and the little cardboard squares. There were only a dozen or so people at the
Badlands Saloon that evening—mostly the regulars, the familiar
faces—and everybody had their drinks and their seats and Kate gave
the old iron cage a good crank.

"G-24," she called out from behind the bar, holding one of the little bingo Ping-Pong balls in her hand.

"BINGO!" Tank hollered out. Kate looked down the bar at him
and just sort of shook her head and smiled that understanding smile
of hers. Tank's head was down flat on top of the bar. He didn't even
have a bingo card in front of him.

"B-14," Kate said, taking another worn white ball from the iron
cage.

"BIIIIIINNNNGGGOOOOO!" Tank screamed, all muffled, his
head buried in his arms on top of the bar, a smoldering cigarette
dangling from his workingman's hand.

"Ah, come on, Tank," Lacy said quietly from across the room. I
turned to look at her and she just smiled back, shaking her head. It
was clear that Lacy had watched Tank sail stormy waters before, and
you could also tell that it was Tank's sloppiness that bothered her the
most. Life was *easy* for Lacy because she lived by a simple, fluid
code—life was just a river, imperfect and meandering, but always
always always finding the ocean. Tank Wilson had a hurricane in his
head.

Willie Beck was standing at the end of the bar studying his bingo
card carefully, as if there might be a hidden code in it somewhere,
some secret design that he hadn't seen before. He was moving his
finger across the little board, side to side and up and down and
diagonally, trying to decipher a rhythm to the letters sweet Kate was
calling out.

"O-22."

"BINGOISAIDGODDAMNIT!!!"

Tank slammed his hand down on the bar with fury and in a flash of miscalculated movement flipped himself over in his bar stool, crashing backward onto the barroom floor with a thud and a loud crack. Everybody at the Badlands Saloon looked over at him lying there, flat on his back on the floor, his legs sticking up into the air toward the ceiling. But nobody was upset or even seemed surprised. Tank Wilson was dazed and half knocked out.

"Bingoisaid," he said quietly under his breath, clumsily picking himself up off the floor, all hunched over like a prehistoric man. He turned and scanned the room slowly for a minute, and then he left, falling through the front door of the Badlands Saloon, out onto Main Street.

Horny Old Crowns

At some point it just got to be too awkward working for Tank Wilson, so I decided to quit my job at Chains & Whistles. And with this move, of course, I needed to find a new place to live because the cozy ambiance of Wigwam came with the job at the bike shop, and in leaving the job, I found myself homeless, too.

I was sitting by myself at the Badlands Saloon after I'd told Tank about my decision to quit, drinking straight whiskey and beer. It was late afternoon and the sun shining through the window caught the smoke coming from my cigarette and made it dance a slow ghost-dance up toward the ceiling, slowly turning and churning like clouds in a canyon. There were a couple of too-loud tourists behind me in a booth jabbering away about nonsense, but otherwise the place was mostly empty. I'd told Kate what had happened—my quitting the bike shop—and she was sympathetic.

Tank was indifferent when I told him I thought I'd just move on. "Gotta do what ya gotta do, buddy-boy," he'd said. It was getting late in the summer—only a couple of weeks left in the season at that point—and Tank Wilson had a bad case of the Fishbowl Blues. Marysville was a beautiful place, but it was isolated—most of the people you talked to each day were only passing through, on their way from one place to another place, and sometimes when you're at that stationary point in-between, it can feel like purgatory.

Big Man was feeling it, too. He and his old lady were close to the breaking point by then and Big Man was spending a lot of time closing down the bars and waking up in the parks, or out behind Chains & Whistles next to Wallingford Creek. He was an absolutely vicious animal when he got drunk because it took enormous amounts of booze and beer to load him up, and when he got there—to the foamy, amber top of the midnight mountain—he was a screaming/snarling son of a bitch.

Willie Beck came hopping into the Badlands Saloon, popped up to the bar and slapped it five times fast with the palms of his hands—*bum-bum-bum-bum-bum.*

"Hi, Willie," Kate said and gave him a hug. She was clearing empty glasses from the tourists' table.

"Hello, Angel," Willie Beck said and swooned dramatically, flashing me a smile. "My lucky day, lucky day." Then he hugged me, too. "How you doin', young feller?"

"Hey, Willie."

"You got the long face," he said, frowning all sarcastically.

I told Willie about my pending homelessness and my unemployment. I leaned in close and told him about Lacy, too, and my guilt trip. He looked at me seriously, through those foggy old glasses of his:

"We all wear the same, horny old crown, m'boy."

Willie Beck patted me on the shoulder and bought me a beer. Then he let out a mighty yalp, up toward the ceiling of the Badlands Saloon: "WHOOOOOOP!"

Willie and I drank beers and intermittent whiskeys for several hours there at the bar. He said things to me like:

"The Bible says to treat your neighbor like yourself. *But sometimes you just can't do that.*"

And:

"Sometimes life is hard, and sometimes it's just funny."

And:

"Every mornin' I wake up, and I'm still alive."

The mayor, Donald Grinhauser, came into the Badlands Saloon with his wife Barbara while Willie and I were chatting at the bar. The summer was winding down and the mayor probably felt compelled to make an appearance at the bar—press some flesh—before things closed down for the season.

"Good afternoon, Mr. Beck," the mayor said to Willie as he passed behind us. The mayor addressed everybody in Marysville formally, by their last names. Or if he didn't know you—if you were a tourist or a seasonal employee like me—he'd just smile that small-town politician's grin of his and nod in recognition, welcoming the out-of-towners to "our fair city," and hoping that the seasonal employees would go out and tell the rest of the world about the "Jewel of the West" when they left.

"Good afternoon yerself, Mr. Grin-Grin-Hauser," Willie said under his breath after the mayor and his wife sat down in one of the high-backed booths across the room. "Grin-Grin-Grin . . . Ha-Ha-Ha . . . Sir-Sir-Sir." Willie Beck pounded the bar and laughed out loud: "HEY-HEY!!" The mayor looked over at me and Willie sitting there at the bar, and then just went on talking to his wife Barbara over cups of coffee.

Later that night all the actors and the tourists were working their way back down into Marysville. The Jigglers came into the Badlands Saloon and Hokey Carmichael joined me and Willie Beck at the bar.

"Gentlemen." Hokey was looking a little bit defeated. It seemed like a lot of folks were wearing down by that point in the summer. I guess the rocky Midwestern wilderness took its toll on a guy after a couple of months. The Jigglers were being booed and shouted off the stage nearly every night that summer up at the amphitheater and it was turning into an exhausting experience for them.

"How was the show tonight?" I asked Hokey.

"Somebody threw a cowboy boot at me tonight while I was onstage juggling *chain saws*."

It had been that sort of an August for the Jigglers.

"You know," he continued, "if we hadn't been doing this for so long, all these years and years on the road doing this show, I think I'd just quit it all right now and get a job behind a desk somewhere. I've really about had it. But I'm pretty much unqualified to do anything else." Kate poured him a shot of whiskey and he drank it and nodded for another. "Ahhhh," he said, putting the empty shot glass upside down onto the bar.

I told Hokey Carmichael about my situation.

"Hell," he said, "you can crash with us."

The Jigglers had rented a large suite for the summer at the Old

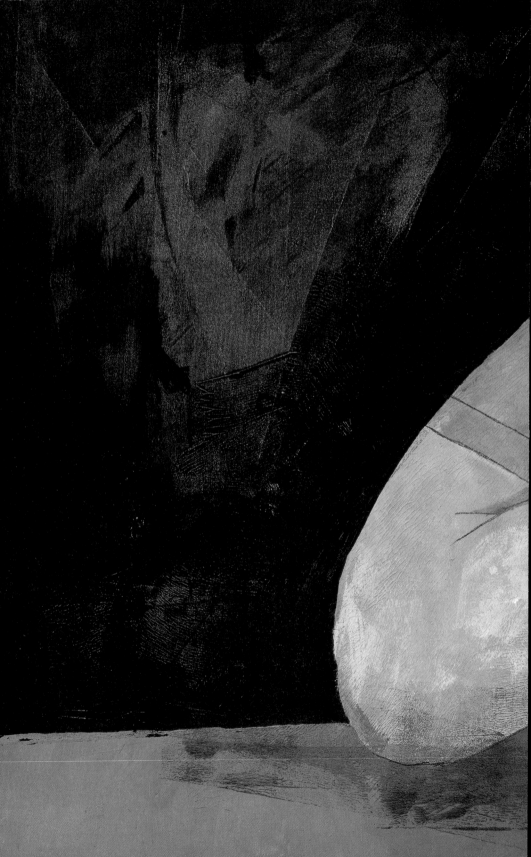

Hotel down the street from the Badlands Saloon—the same place where Lacy lived.

"Should we ask the other guys?" I asked him.

"Nah," Hokey said, looking over at Hank Langhorne and Fritz across the room. "You can sleep on the couch."

There were only a couple of weeks left that summer and finding a place to live was the first of my challenges. The other one—that ever-present, tick-tock question—was still hanging there in the air over my head like Damocles's sword: *How are you going to make a living?* That was the never-ending question, and I didn't have a clue.

The door to the bar slammed open and Big Man—Ralphy Williams—came barreling in, limping and hopping, hooting and hollering like a man in a gorilla costume, scratching at his armpits and moaning and shaking his head back and forth like he was in heat. He took an unattended glass of beer from a table there by the door and drank and screamed out all primitive and started shaking his head again. The bar was relatively full by that time and the jukebox was blaring loud, but everybody in the place turned around and stared at him for a second. Big Man leaned back and screamed— "WHHAAAAAA!"—pounding on his chest, a real King Kong routine. He lurched over to me at the bar and got regular for a second:

"This afternoon the bitch told me I was an apish brute," he said. "So here I am. The monkey's outta the cage."

He rolled his eyes back into his head and started hollering again, running around the barroom in circles, flailing his arms and grunting. He grabbed hold of the mayor and tried to dry-hump his leg. Kate screamed out from behind the bar: "RALPH!"

"GOOD JESUS, MR. WILLIAMS! GRAB HOLD OF YOUR-SELF!!" Mayor Donald Grinhauser implored, spilling lukewarm coffee all over the place.

Ralphy stood up, Homo sapiens style, and walked calmly over to the bar. "Hi, Kate. How are you doing this fine evening? Whiskey, please."

Kate took a glass from behind the bar and started filling it with ice, but Big Man stopped her. "No, Kate," he said, slapping a fifty-dollar bill down onto the bar. "The whole bottle, darling."

Kate looked at me and then over at Big Man. "You can't drink it here, Ralphy," she said.

"I wouldn't think of it, Katie. This is no place for an animal like me," he said, taking the bottle. "Good evening, humanoids."

Big Man walked out of the Badlands Saloon, cool as a cardplayer. All of his chips were in.

Sweet Kate flipped the lights on as the last song faded from the jukebox. Everybody had gone home and the remnants of the night were strewn about the room like memories, empty pitchers of beer and lipstick-stained whiskey glasses covered the tables, black plastic ashtrays overflowing with fag-ends and ashes. A mist of cigarette smoke still hung around the ceiling in the hot barroom air. It was an aftermath of sorts, but none of it was anything new. Kate shuffled around the room clearing the glasses—five to a hand—humming some tune to herself.

"Another night in the scorebook, huh?" I said to her as she dropped the empty glasses and pitchers into a sinkful of soapy water behind the bar.

"Yeah," she said, smiling that weary late-night smile of hers.

The only other person left in the place was Willie Beck, leaning back in a chair with his feet up on the pool table, smoking a cigarette and looking out over the room, deep in thought. That's pretty much how Willie ended every night at the Badlands Saloon: Pensively—not so much melancholy as thoughtful and reflective, a simple philosopher trying to figure it all out, knowing full well that he didn't have the tools.

I wondered about Willie Beck then, sitting back there contently by himself after closing time at the Badlands Saloon, looking so satisfied, on some level, or at least resigned to the general restlessness of life. *What did Willie Beck worry about when he was all alone in his trailer park trailer in the middle of the night? Did Willie Beck ever worry about anything? Did Willie Beck ever worry about dying? Did Willie Beck believe in heaven or hell?*

I suppose he thought about all of those things at one time or another, because those kinds of questions were just too human not to. But Willie Beck seemed to have found a rhythm in life that worked for him—he'd made a pact with God or nature or whatever it was that Willie Beck ultimately answered to, an agreement that life, in the end, made no sense at all.

Willie Beck stood up there at the back of the barroom with a third of a pitcher of beer in his hand, said "Hey-yup" to me and Kate and walked out the backdoor of the Badlands Saloon.

"Where's he going?" I asked Kate.

"Oh, that's how he gets home sometimes when he's the last one to leave." Kate smiled and shook her head. "You ought to go and watch him out there. It's a stitch what he's doing."

I set my empty glass down, walked over to the screened door at the back of the barroom and stepped out into the pitch darkness there behind the Badlands Saloon.

"Willie?" I half whispered.

"Hey-yup." I heard Willie Beck before I could see him. The sound of his voice came from someplace down by my feet, or below that, even. "Good times tonight, eh young feller?" My eyes were slowly dilating and I could just start to make out Willie Beck's yellow shirt there below me, floating away down Wallingford Creek.

"Willie?" I said again as the image started to reveal itself.

"G'night, young feller."

Willie Beck was floating away down Wallingford Creek on his back, fully clothed, sipping beer from a plastic pitcher, his soaked loafers pointing up toward the stars. The creek ran out of town—out past the trailer park where Willie and Llewelyn lived—but it hardly seemed like a logical way to get home. Willie Beck was happily illogical, though, and he raised his pitcher in my direction as he faded into the dark night, a surreal walrus making the old commute.

Souvenirs

I woke up the next morning in the Jigglers' suite at the Old Hotel. Empty beer cans and plastic cups full of cigarette butts covered almost every available flat surface in the place. The suite had a real fraternity house ambiance—dirty laundry and candy wrappers all over the place, an incense jar with a half-eaten sandwich shoved into it. The Jigglers were road warriors, after all, and they never got too caught up in the details—their living quarters weren't a *home,* just a messy stop along the way.

Hokey Carmichael, Hank Langhorne and Fritz were all still sleeping when I woke up so I let myself out. I walked down to the south side of Marysville—careful to avoid Main Street and Chains & Whistles—and grabbed a coffee at the coffee shop in the little strip mall there. The coffee still tasted bloody and raw to me but it was coffee, anyway, and I walked on out of town drinking that iron-flavored brew, down the familiar road that led out to the trailer park and Wigwam.

Willie Beck was sitting on the front steps of his trailer as I passed by, cleaning out a pipe.

"Hey, Willie," I said. "What's the news?"

"Heh-heh! Pipe-cleanin' time," he said. "You movin' out today, I s'pose . . ."

"Yeah," I said as I walked by. "I'm gonna move my things over to the Old Hotel for the next couple of weeks before I head back to New York. The Jigglers are putting me up."

"The Jigglers," Willie Beck said, giggling. He looked up at me and then he laughed out loud: "HA!"

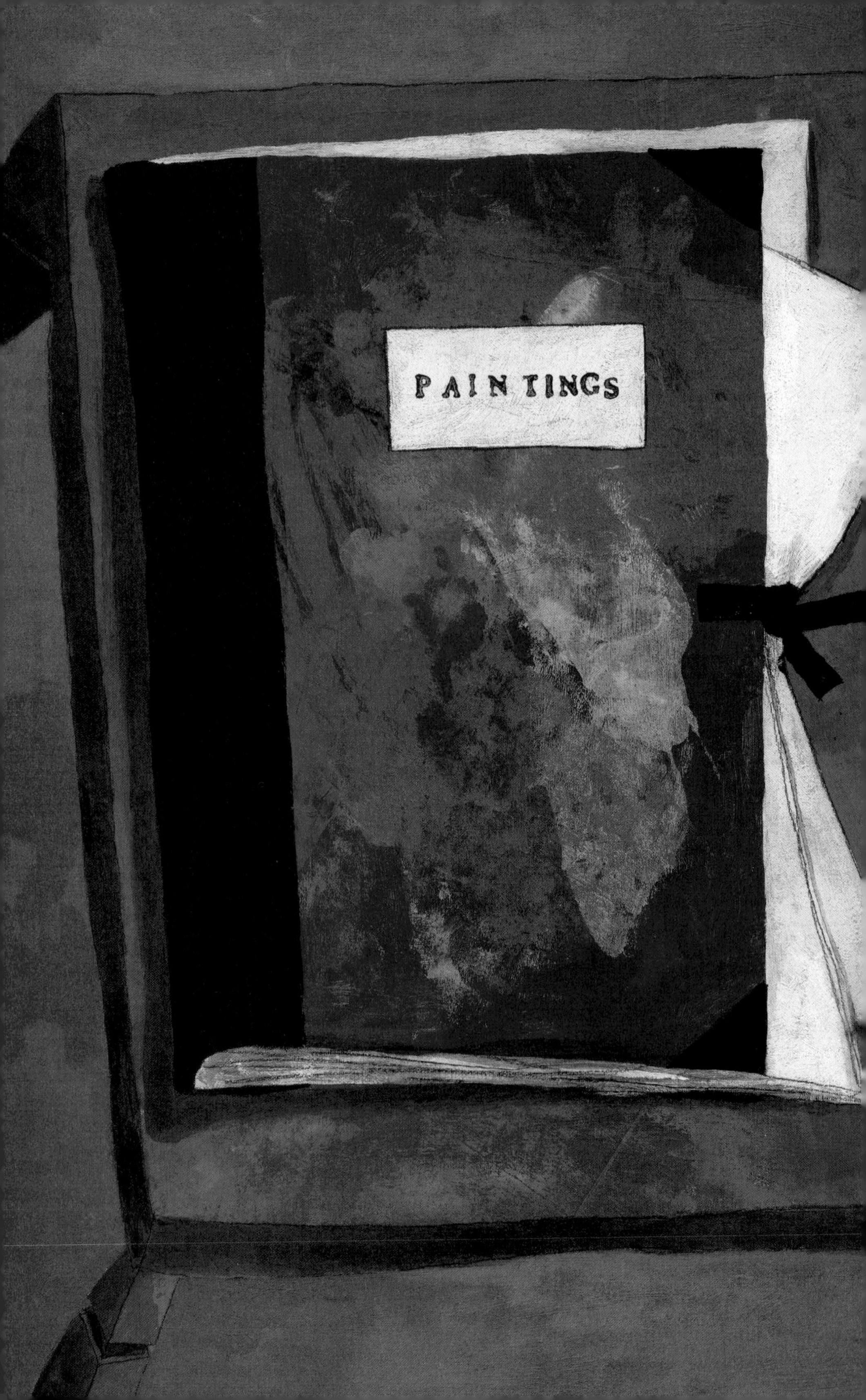
PAINTINGS

Willie seemed a little sad to see me go and I had to admit I wasn't too excited about it, either. Aside from the lonely, silent midnights, I'd come to feel at home there at Wigwam. I walked up the rickety wooden steps and took the key from around my neck—I kept it tied there on a little piece of string—and when I put the key into the shaky little front-door knob of the trailer it made a sad sound. I went in and shut the door behind me. A mouse squirted across the linoleum of the kitchen and disappeared underneath the sink. I stood there in the silent afternoon half-light for a couple of minutes just looking around, remembering my first day there at Wigwam at the beginning of the summer: *"Let me forget about today until tomorrow . . ."*

Most of the paintings I'd done that summer were taped to the fake wood-paneled walls, pictures of Smoochie and the hills, single-speed bicycles and Mildred Zimmerman, a lonely little white ghost-dog that hung around the Badlands Saloon at night, pictures of Big Man and Tank Wilson, Colonel James Lawrence and his family, and Lacy. I started collecting all the tools of my trade into the canvas satchel I'd brought them in from New York City, the brushes and pens, the inks and the acrylics. I carefully took the paintings down from the walls and rolled them up together and stuck them into a cardboard tube I'd found on the street in Marysville. I went to the back of the trailer to the bedroom—the bedroom I'd only spent half of one night in—my first night—and folded the few pairs of jeans and T-shirts and shorts I had there.

It was all a strange feeling, like I was leaving before I'd actually left, an almost out-of-body experience, like I was watching myself already from some other place. There were still a couple of weeks left before I had to head over to Dickinson to catch the plane that'd take me back to New York City by way of Minneapolis, but my Bad-lands summer was coming to an end and I'd always hated good-byes, any kind of good-byes, even the small ones—saying good-bye to my mom at the Bismarck airport, knowing that I'd see her again, but also knowing that nothing is for sure, watching her cry a little bit as I walked away. Those little things always tore me up, and packing everything up at Wigwam made me feel sentimental and lonesome, because my time there was done.

I was closing up my suitcase in the living room at Wigwam when somebody knocked on the door. *Who's that?* I hoped it wasn't Tank Wilson, or even Lacy. I opened the door.

"Hey, young feller, you need a hand?"

It was Willie Beck.

"Willie. Yeah, come on in."

Willie and I'd always had an unspoken gentleman's agreement that our homes were our castles, a little slice of privacy in a town where everybody knew everything about everybody else. I'd certainly never been inside his and Llewelyn's trailer—had never even met Llewelyn that whole summer long—but it was a comfortable understanding and it worked.

"Nice place you got here," he said, standing there in the living room of Wigwam. "And clean, too. HEH!"

Willie was wearing the same yellow polyester shirt and the same pair of brown polyester pants he was wearing the night I met him earlier that summer. His shirt pockets were cram-packed with a case for his glasses and a pipe and tobacco and several pens and a number-two pencil.

"I've got to walk all this stuff over to the Old Hotel," I told him. "You sure you want to go all that way?" I really didn't have much to carry, just the old suitcase with my clothes and the canvas satchel with my supplies, and the paintings and the drawings and the sketchbooks I'd accumulated there that summer.

"Hey-yup," he said without hesitating and grabbed the suitcase.

"Okay," I said. "Thanks, Willie."

I opened the door for him and then just stood there for a second again by myself, looking back on the front room there at Wigwam, trying to burn it all into my mind.

We started walking, me and Willie Beck, past his trailer and on through the campground there next to the little trailer park, down the old gravel road that led past the swimming pool to the paved main road that would take us back into Marysville. It was only a mile, at best, and we walked it silently, me and Willie Beck, hugging the shoulder of the road as we went along, our shoes crunching the gravel on the lip of the ditch. It was overcast that afternoon and for a split second in time me and Willie Beck were bygone hobos—hitch-hikers—without a thought of trying to flag down a ride.

When we got to the Old Hotel in Marysville, I thanked Willie Beck. "I can get it from here," I said. "Thanks, Willie."

"Hey-yup," he said, patting me on the shoulder. "You're good to go, now." He looked me straight in the eye tenderly for a split second, over the top of those foggy horn-rimmed glasses of his, and then he turned and walked across the street, shrinking away into the late-day Marysville afternoon. I watched him for a minute, bopping along there the way he always did—half dancing, half hopping—until he disappeared into the Badlands Saloon and was gone.

I kept looking across the street at the Badlands Saloon after Willie Beck had disappeared, trying to freeze-frame that moment. People always say how fast life goes by and they're almost right, because most of the time the basic day-to-day goings-on in this world are fast and forgettable—the dish-washing and the bill-paying and the traffic-jamming and the general waiting, waiting, waiting. But there are those moments—little, seemingly insignificant moments—that pop up sometimes and you just want to grab hold of those visions and keep them somehow, lock them away in some pristine place, because you know that someday you'll need them.

Funny Faces

How do you make a living making paintings and drawings? That question had taken on a real urgency for me at that point in my Badlands summer, because even though I'd found a place to lay my head each night with the Jigglers at the Old Hotel, there were still a couple of weeks left that summer and I needed to earn money. *Money, money, money.* New York City was an expensive town and I couldn't afford to go back east empty-handed.

I thought back to my summers while I was an undergraduate, traveling around the Upper Midwest, drawing distorted cartoon portraits at outdoor art festivals, and how that had floated my boat back then, at least financially. Maybe something like that could work there in Marysville? There were plenty of tourists, and they weren't renting bicycles.

I went downstairs in the Old Hotel, out back to the alley and the garbage Dumpsters there and found—miraculously—a nearly clean sheet of cardboard, four-foot square. I hauled it back up to the suite and opened up my kit bag with all the inks and pens and brushes and paints and proceeded to make my sign—my storefront, really, an on-the-spot advertisement. I grabbed some of the various magazines the Jigglers had lying around the living room and tore out pictures of celebrities and otherwise well-known people: A couple of presidents and a few movie stars, one or two Rock-and-Roll personalities, half a dozen other recognizable members of the paparazzi scene. And I drew them all, pen-and-ink and watercolor on sheets of sketchbook paper. The ink really flew, one face after the other, over and over again until I got each ear, nose and throat just distorted enough to still be recognizable. I drew for hours there on the coffee table in the living room of the Jigglers suite at the Old Hotel, every care or worry I'd ever had in the world made tangible in the abstract marks on the page, and then obliterated completely—transcended, destroyed, conquered—until I had a dozen finished portraits, a little gallery that I assembled on my salvaged square of cardboard. Below the drawings, with red and black markers, I printed: *YOUR CARICA-TURE IN UNDER TEN MINUTES!!!* And then: *BLACK & WHITE: $7; COLOR: $10.*

I leaned the sign up against a chair and stood back, looking at it for a couple of minutes, satisfied. I packed up my tools, grabbed the sign and left the Old Hotel. It was just past midday.

I'd never been a performer and the idea of setting a couple of lawn chairs up on the street somewhere in Marysville with my fresh carica-ture advertising sign terrified me. But then my lower middle-class roots kicked in: *You've got to earn a living, buddy-boy.*

Down the street from the Old Hotel, toward the southern edge of town, was Marysville's little amusement boardwalk—the Old West Shooting Gallery, the bumper cars and the miniature golf course. The musical up at the amphitheater didn't start for a couple of hours and a few of the chartered buses that ferried in each night's audience were docked out in front of the shooting gallery, so I decided to set myself up there. On the north side of the shooting gallery was a small park area with benches and a little fountain with a concrete buffalo. I leaned my homemade sign up against one of the benches there and then set up the two lawn chairs, one facing the other. I sat down in one of the chairs and took out a pad of watercolor paper and a jar of ink and my favorite pen and started doodling around, just trying to calm down my nerves and lose myself for a second or two. I drew a tree in the little park, and then the bench across the way from me. I drew a nice picture of the con-crete buffalo in the middle of the fountain, the beast's head thrown back majestically into the air, water spraying out of his mouth in a steady stream up toward the Badlands sky. I thought about that mid-night herd of buffalo up at Cottonwood Campground with Hubert Summerlin, and wondered if Hubert had ever made it out to Seattle in his old green pickup truck.

As I drew the concrete buffalo a little girl who couldn't have been more than nine or ten years old wandered over behind me and looked over my shoulder while I worked. And that's the funny thing when you're making a drawing—people don't know that you know they're watching.

"Hi," I said after awhile. "Can you tell what it is?"

The little girl looked over at the buffalo in the fountain and then at the drawing on the page and smiled.

"Yeah," I said. "That's him."

I doodled the drawing awhile longer and then I turned around. The little girl was shy when I turned to look at her, like a spell had been broken.

"What's your name?"

"Lilly," she said, looking down at her socks and sandals. Lilly's dad ran the shooting gallery and the bumper cars each summer.

"Do you like to draw, Lilly?" I asked her.

"Yeeeaaahhh," she said, all shy and drawn-out, fidgeting with her baby-blue dress.

"I've got an idea," I said. "Maybe I could draw a picture of you?"

"Okay," she said. She was excited, but a little bit cautious, too. "I have to ask my daddy first."

Lilly's little legs flew across the boardwalk and around the corner of the shooting gallery to where her father was working. Above the tings and pops of the tourists and their pellet guns I heard Lilly ask her father: "Daddy! Daddy! There's a man in the park drawing pictures and he wants to draw a picture of me!" Lilly's father poked his head around the corner of the building and eyed me for a second, smiled and disappeared. I heard him say something, but I couldn't make out what it was. Lilly came tearing out of the shooting gallery with an ecstatic smile on her face.

"MY DADDY SAID YOU CAN DRAW ME!" she half screamed and climbed into the lawn chair across from me. Her father poked his head around the corner of the building again. I gave him a little wink and he smiled again.

There's an innocence and cautious sense of safety in small towns like Marysville. Bad things happen everywhere and tragedy knows no borders, but in Marysville a person just felt *safe*. There was a quiet optimism in watching little Lilly roam around on a sunny, cloudless summer afternoon in Marysville, making up games and exploring her world unafraid. It sometimes seemed to me that the world had gotten ahead of itself, too overly complicated for something so simple as being young and bored on a small-town Saturday afternoon.

Lilly was a patient model. She sat there frozen in that old lawn chair, perfectly still while I worked. "What do you like to do for fun, Lilly?" I asked her as I drew. Her legs were too short for the lawn chair and they stuck straight out toward me. She rested her arms on the chair's aluminum armrests, looking like a humble little North Dakota queen in a too-big throne.

"We have horses. My horse's name is Beauty and I can ride her all by myself. My brother Jack's horse's name is Funny, but Jack's too little to ride Funny all by himself."

"Your brother's horse's name is *Funny*?" I asked her.

"Yeah," she said.

"That's a funny name for a horse," I said and Lilly giggled for a second and then got straight-faced again and sat perfectly still.

I drew Lilly riding an imaginary black stallion, a cowgirl's hat on her head and pretty pink cowgirl boots on her feet. I put a lasso in her hand and a bright yellow sun in the sky.

As I finished the drawing I noticed Lilly looking past me, over my shoulder. I turned around and there was a crowd of ten or twelve people gathered there—mostly senior citizens with perfectly quaffed blue-silver hairdos. I turned back to Lilly and showed her the finished drawing. She squealed with glee and jumped down from her lawn chair. I tore the drawing from my block of paper and handed it to her. "Be careful," I said, "some of the ink might still be wet."

Lilly took the drawing from me carefully and sprinted around the corner of the shooting gallery yelling, "Daddy-Daddy-Daddy!!!"

I looked up over my shoulder at the old crowd standing above me. "Who's next?" I said. They all started to jostle and huff around uncomfortably.

"You should do it, Joanne," one of them said to her friend.

"Bill, why don't you sit down?"

A real silver-haired dandy walked over to the empty lawn chair across from me, all Wranglers and Western Grit. He was wearing a perfectly fitted custom-made Stetson hat. "Take it easy on me, son," he said. "And why don't you make it in color."

I couldn't have imagined a better model than this weathered old ranch hand. He sat there in front of me nervously while I drew, laughing occasionally at the looks on the faces of his friends standing behind me. The tip of my pen hooked the edge of the sheet of paper and splattered ink across the page.

"Whoops," the old man said. "I guess you made a mistake."

"Nope," I said. "There aren't any mistakes here."

His friends and his wife laughed out loud behind me and hung on every mark I made, every crosshatch and scribble. When I finished the drawing everybody behind me started clapping and laughing and jibing my cowboy sitter.

"Well I'll be damned," he said when I showed him the finished drawing. "If it wasn't so good I'd punch you in the nose." He paid me the ten dollars and forced a buddy of his down into the empty lawn chair. "Draw this guy," he said. "Shouldn't be hard to make him look ugly!" he said and everyone laughed again behind me.

I drew for five hours straight that first day—children and their parents, whole busloads of tourists and a handful of locals, too, everybody done-up and distorted, everybody having a good time. I made more money those first five hours than I did working a whole week at Chains & Whistles and that felt good, like there was *hope*. Or like my dad always told me back there in those sweet halcyon days of Bismarck: "You'll never starve, Oliver."

Sunday Comes After Saturday

190   *the telephone ringin' hurts this mornin'. THE GODDAMNED NOISE!! i shouldn't curse on Sunday mornin' though, i s'pose. it's lacy and larry callin' me too early in the mornin'. what time is it? trailer-paintin' time it sounds like. they said they'd put a coat of paint on the old trailer. (heh.) nice kids. i s'pose I told them it was ok. does the old trailer really need paintin'? is my trailer worn out? oh, the wind and the rain. (heh.) i know llewelyn doesn't care, one way or the other. i don't really care, either. appearances appearances appearances. (heh-heh.) got the headache this mornin'. should i take a couple of aspirin? what about the stomach bleeding?* "IF YOU CONSUME 3 OR MORE ALCOHOLIC DRINKS EVERY DAY, ASK YOUR DOCTOR WHETHER YOU SHOULD TAKE THIS PILL OR OTHER PAIN REDUCERS. THIS PILL MAY CAUSE LIVER DAMAGE." *that's what it says on the bottle. jesus. should i do it? i don't want the liver damage. my momma had the ulcers. llewelyn has 'em, too. what hurts worse, the ulcers or the liver damage? jesus. these labels will scare the hell out of a guy. whoops. i probably shouldn't curse. it's sunday. sunday comes after saturday. (heh.) i'm not gonna worry about it. i couldn't even eat a potato chip at the moment anyway. (heh-heh.) ouch. head hurts this mornin'. good times last night, but hard times this mornin'. what day is it? sunday mornin' comin' down. should i put on pants today? nope. sunday's the day to rest, the bible says. puttin' on pants is hard work on sundays. i think i shot good pool last night. did i win? i can't really remember. probably not. but i had fun, yes sir. did somebody win? does it matter? i hope so. can there be a winner at the badlands saloon? (heh.) ouch. hurts to laugh in my head this mornin'. yes. there are always winners and sometimes a few losers but the rules always seem to get changed up and I can't ever figure out why. potato chips? (heh-heh.)*

ouch. i like the young folks. full of goddamned life. shit. whoops. i shouldn't swear on sundays. i was young yesterday. feels like it. only difference is now the hurt doesn't hurt so bad. same hurt in a different way. am i a philosopher? (heh-heh.) ouch. when was the last time i went to church? when momma died. i miss my momma. i remember when she died. i remember when she died. i remember when she died. she was a good little lady. i still got llewelyn, though, i s'pose. but llewelyn snores.

"YESHELLO!!??" phone-ringin'-sound hurts like hell this mornin'. "YES!" it's that beautiful girl lacy who the young feller likes so much. "I ALREADY TOLD YOU YES IT'S ALRIGHT TO COME OVER AND PAINT THE GODDAMNED PLACE!!" ouchgod. whoops. shouldn't swear. "yes, thank you guys i love you." lacy and larry callin' on the telephone and the telephone hurts this mornin'. the ringer's too loud. lacy and larry really want to paint the old trailer today, i guess. charity work? maybe lacy and larry don't get hangovers. i get 'em sometimes but they're different now. different kind of hurt now. wish i could get day-overs instead. like do-overs. i wish i was in the fifth grade again. i remember the first time i fell in love. sweet little blond-headed little girl named nancy. you never forget your first love, do you? (heh.) ouch. why didn't i get married? (heh-heh.) funny question. i used to think about that question a lot but i don't think about that question so much anymore. what would llewelyn do without me? (heh.) llewelyn's not my wife, he's my brother. llewelyn is my brother and i love him. is it too early for a beer? nope. it's past lunchtime, i s'pose. i slept in today with the headache. it's time for potato chips and a beer.

the sun feels like heaven this afternoon. is this heaven? (heh.) yes. for now, this is heaven. lacy and larry are doin' a good job on the trailer over there, good silver paintin' job. good kids. i thank them. llewelyn's still snorin' inside the trailer—i can hear him even way out here in the yard. i like lawn chairs. i like this lawn chair i'm sittin' in right now. it's an old lawn chair but i like it. it feels like forever-home right now. i like this beer i'm drinkin', too, here in this glass in my hand and i like that little water sprinkler there on the lawn. there's a little rainbow in the water comin' from it there. (heh-heh.) i almost feel like i can hear organ music playin' somewhere right now. is there a show up at the amphitheater this afternoon? nope. it's sunday afternoon. the shows up at the amphitheater are every night in the summer-times, not in the afternoons, but i can hear beautiful music like waves right

now, or like a rhythm—no voices just beautiful beautiful beautiful music,
organ music, maybe from someplace else? yes. from someplace else. i love this
music. it's warm and it's summertime. is this what it feels like? yes. yes. yes.
this is what it feels like. it feels like home. i'm home.

Dream-Powered Wings

Those last two weeks in Marysville were a revelation in a lot of ways.
The Jigglers were honest roommates, if a little bit sloppy. They took
me in graciously as an honorary fourth member of their juggling
gang for the rest of the summer according to some road code, making me feel right at home at a time when I felt like a leaf without a
tree. And each day I'd set up my rickety little lawn chairs and my
homemade sign next door to the Old West Shooting Gallery and
draw caricatures of all the tourists, the young kids and the senior citizens, short people and tall people, folks with big noses and strangers
with wild eyes. I must've drawn five hundred goofy-looking faces those
last two weeks alone, sitter after sitter, black-and-white and color, ink
flying all over the place, lots of smiles and big laughter. I made one little boy cry, though, and I felt bad about that—I'd put a big belly on
this little boy's body in the drawing and when I showed him the finished picture the tears just rolled and rolled down his plump, rosy
cheeks and his mother hissed at me: "Can't you see that he has a
weight problem!" She threw the ten bucks onto my drawing board
anyway and grabbed her pubbly little crying child and stormed off
and I felt bad about that one, but that one was the exception that
summer because everybody loved laughing at themselves when it was
no fault of their own, just God-given looks and exaggerated exaggera-
tions, the way whiskers can even be funny sometimes, or double chins.

Little Lilly hung out with me every afternoon, too, watching me
draw with all of her small-town enthusiasm. Lilly loved watching me
work—hanging over my shoulder like a little lieutenant on sniper
watch—and when I signed each drawing after it was finished she

would jump up and down, giggling and clapping her hands like it was all the best magic she'd ever seen.

That last day of the season I packed up my caricature gear early, next door to the Old West Shooting Gallery. The tourist trade was winding down there in Marysville and things were getting quiet, like a cool wind coming in that marked the changing of the seasons. I headed back to the Old Hotel to get my things together. Hokey Carmichael and Hank Langhorne and Fritz had already left for their last show up at the amphitheater that evening and the suite was, in its own funky way, serene. I grabbed a beer from the refrigerator and sat down by myself on the crusty old couch in the living room and just exhaled for a second, as the summer came to a head.

I was a sentimental character and I was sad to be leaving Marysville, but I was also deeply satisfied on some level, sitting there on the sofa at the Old Hotel. Because in a Marysville kind of way, *I'd made it.* Drawing pictures had saved my Badlands summer. Writers and artists talk about the terror of the blank page, the way an untouched piece of paper or canvas can cripple the creative juices—freeze up the machinery like a deer in God's headlights—but I'd never felt that way. I'd never felt that way at all. The blank page was *freedom* to me, a perfect world waiting to be defined. The finished work might very well be imperfect—in fact it more likely than not would be imperfect—but for that brief moment before the pen hits the paper or the loaded brush mars the blank canvas, it's a perfect world waiting to be born. None of it made any sense at all, but that feeling—that eternal possibility—set me free.

I finished my beer and walked downstairs in the Old Hotel and out onto the street. It was a calm, crystal-clear evening deep in August and I started walking south, out of town, up the gravel road there to where the off-road trail began. I'd given my bike back to Tank Wilson a couple of weeks earlier so I hadn't been up in those hills around Marysville for a while and I wanted to see the view from up there one more time before I left town.

I crossed the ditch at the top of the hill, passed through the barbed-wire fence and on into the back country, down a few gullies and back up again and then up again still, to the top of a wind-washed sandstone butte where I could see everything I wanted to see. I sat down on that ancient ground, took hold of my knees and rested my chin there, the sun closing in on the horizon by then, the air still, like in a vacuum. I could see all the way down to South Dakota, out west to Montana and maybe even Canada to the north, but I couldn't be sure. Marysville down below me looked so little, like it was a pretend town or even just a sunset dream. Marysville was a tiny little town in the middle of nowhere, *but was it really that small?* It had been my whole world for those three months, my home, my entire *universe.* Willie Beck was down there somewhere, and so was Lacy, probably playing a game of pool at the Badlands Saloon or looking for a few more agates over at the quarry before it got too dark, another late-day grab for that beautiful native girl. Any place looks small when you put some distance between it and yourself— even New York City—but there aren't any burnt-umber ancient dinosaur buttes in New York City. The views there are different.

I looked over my shoulder to the east, sitting there on top of the North Dakota world. Those clouds hanging out there in that cerulean blue sky a hundred miles away were looking down on Bismarck, looking down on my mom and my dad and my little brother, all of my yesterdays and all of my loves, the little streets and schoolyards that were my *home.* And I remembered a dream I'd had one night at Wigwam that summer: It was a flying dream where I was powered by some dream-powered wings, soaring silently through the midnight above the Missouri River and Bismarck, a hundred feet above that cold, black water there in the cold air and the clouds. I was warm because I was home but the air was still cold because I was all alone, up there in the dream sky where nobody but you can see what you're seeing and nobody but you can feel what you're feeling. Absolute isolation. I landed in my dream flight on the back lawn of my parents' house and walked into their house in the dark of the night while they slept, through the back-porch door. Nobody knew I was there, but I was there. I was there. I walked down the hall of the house to the room where I'd grown up but the door to the room was locked. I heard somebody snoring somewhere and I ran out of the house, back out into that dark misty dream night. I ran ran ran out of the house and outside I tried to remember how to fly again but it was the middle of the night and I was alone and I was afraid.

But I was home.

Lawn Chairs

I woke up on the couch at the Old Hotel. The Jigglers were still sleeping and dreaming away but it was time for me to move, time to say good-bye to old Marysville and those beautiful Badlands, the easy people and the tourists, the gravel roads, the bike trails and the phantom-rattlesnakes. It was time to go back East, back to New York City and whatever might lie ahead for me there in that rattle-clack never-knowing madness, my life sprawled out like a blank sheet of paper.

I finished packing my things and left a note for the Jigglers on the kitchen countertop. I thanked them for their hospitality and I made a little drawing from memory for them, too, a drawing of Hokey Carmichael and Fritz and Hank Langhorne juggling their custom-made juggling clubs on that lonely old stage up there at the amphitheater beneath those cold, unforgiving lights. Everything was in order. I still had a few hours, though, before the shuttle bus would stop on Main Street in front of Chains & Whistles to whisk me away, over to Dickinson and that jet plane that would roar away over Bismarck at thirty thousand feet, to Minneapolis and then LaGuardia Airport and that magnificent New York City and all those animated buildings and crowds of people.

I grabbed my bags—my simple suitcase and all of the drawings and paintings I'd made that summer. I left the Old Hotel, crossed the street and walked down the block to the Badlands Saloon. There were a few people I wanted to say good-bye to, maybe have a couple of early-afternoon drinks in that familiar room, those red vinyl bar stools and that Labrador wallpaper. I wanted to give Kate a big hug and maybe see Larry or Mildred or maybe even Lacy because I still couldn't get her out of my mind, but I especially wanted to shake Willie Beck's hand one more time and buy him a drink, thank him for the hat and wish him good luck.

The Badlands Saloon was quiet that Tuesday afternoon—a smoky barroom afternoon half-light—but the stools at the bar there were full of the regulars—completely full—there wasn't an empty stool or chair or red vinyl booth seat to be had at the Badlands Saloon that afternoon. The place was packed, but everything was dead-quiet.

I walked around to the end of the bar and said "Hey" to Kate who was quietly washing beer glasses and warming slices of pizza in the tiny toaster oven back there behind the bar. "Have you seen Willie?" I asked her casually. "I'm leaving today and I wanted to say goodbye." I was smiling and happy because I loved Marysville, had loved those three months there. Sweet Kate looked up at me from behind the bar with sad eyes. She put down her washrag and came out from behind the bar, stared at me straight, smiling sadly, tilting her head to the side.

"I wish I didn't have to be the one to tell you," she said looking down at her boots, shaking her head slowly back and forth. "Willie died on Sunday."

Willie died on Sunday. Willie died on Sunday. Willie died on Sunday. I wasn't sure I'd heard her right. I couldn't have. I looked down the bar there at the Badlands Saloon, all slow motion, another dream except not a dream, all those old people sitting there on a Tuesday afternoon in their Sunday-best—polyester suits and floral-print dresses, neckties and Stetsons and gold rings, perfume and cologne, but none of the usual Badlands Saloon revelry. I hadn't even really noticed them when I came in—the way everybody was all dressed-up and solemn, the unusual formality there at the Badlands Saloon that unassuming Tuesday afternoon. I thought everyone was just *there.* And they *were* all just there, but they were there for a reason, and they'd heard me ask Kate about Willie Beck and they all sort of looked over their shoulders at me in a vague unison, and then they turned away and looked back again into those mirrors behind the bar.

"Larry and Lacy were painting Willie's trailer on Sunday," Kate told me. "Willie was sitting in a lawn chair there in his yard in his

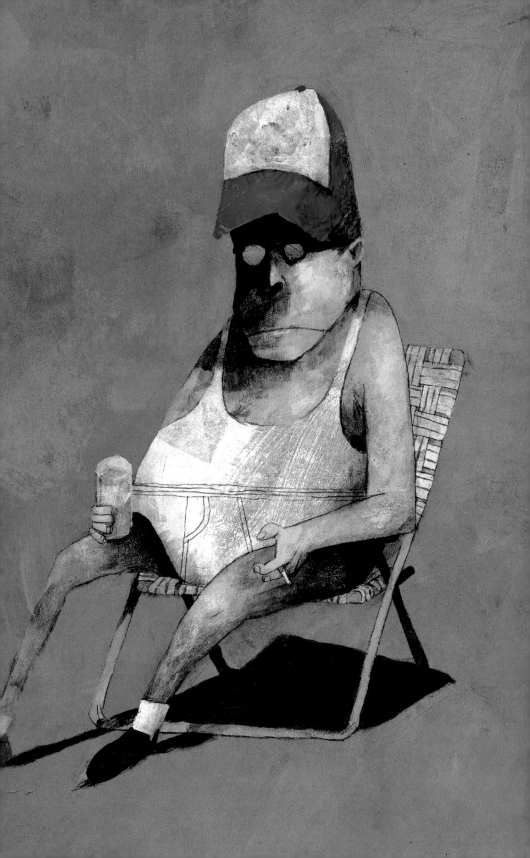

underwear, like he liked to do on Sunday afternoons in the summertime, drinking his beer and getting some sun. They thought he'd fallen asleep," she said, "so they finished painting his house." Kate told me all of this so sympathetically, like a mother or a grandmother, like it was hurting me more than it hurt her to tell it. "When they went over to check on him—to tell him that he had a fresh coat of paint—he was gone. He was still holding half a glass of beer in his hand and an unlit cigarette in his mouth, but he was gone." Beautiful Kate was holding back, trying to keep things matter-of-fact. "His funeral was this morning."

Kate started to cry a little bit. I looked down the bar again at those small-town men and women lined up there, dressed up in their own simple ways—veterans, lovers and friends. Willie Beck was no relative of mine. I'd only known him for a summer of late nights. But he was my *friend*.

Willie Beck was my friend.

That morning they'd buried him in a little prairie cemetery outside of Marysville, up on a hill next to his momma. A photocopied program from his funeral service was sitting there next to an ashtray on top of the bar. It had been a simple burial because Willie Beck didn't have much money and he'd never been interested in long, drawn-out testimonials, but Willie Beck had a lot of friends and they were all there when the time had come to usher him home.

I'd gone back to North Dakota because I thought I was unique at the time, a young man who didn't know what might lay ahead in life, at a crossroads where none of the trails up ahead were marked, where nothing was guaranteed—no profession was secured and the potential for failure was a real possibility. I did what I suppose was instinctual—I went *home*, where all the faces looked familiar and all the license plates were from the same place as me. But an interesting thing happens as we cross that foggy line between adolescence and some kind of adulthood: One random day you look into your own father's eyes and understand that he's no different from you—a father, but just a *man*, too, just a man, like you, fighting all those same struggles that you've ever experienced in your young little life, fought them all ten times over again by the time you even arrived. Maybe that's what I ultimately learned that summer, spending so much time with those good people at the Badlands Saloon: It seemed to me, after everything was said and done, that nobody in Marysville knew what any of it meant either, and that, ultimately, was the *answer*. Mildred Zimmerman and Lacy and Larry and Mel and Jimmy Threepence and everybody else went to the Badlands Saloon to commiserate, simple as that, because in the end that's about all any of us can do. Our fates are wholly individual things, but in that, we're bound together, too, all of us riding complicated trains on parallel tracks.

I thought about all of this on the plane somewhere over Illinois. I'd ordered a whiskey from the flight attendant and she asked to see my ID. "Thanks," she said, handing me back my card. "You look so young."

I took my portfolio down from the overhead compartment and thumbed through the drawings and paintings I'd made that summer: The Badlands Saloon and Wigwam out there west of town; Tank Wilson and beautiful beautiful beautiful Lacy; the Fourth of July parade through old Marysville; Smoochie's desperate midnight ride and Jimmy Threepence singing his old English drinking songs in the middle of the busy barroom; Mildred Zimmerman with her feather boa and those superstar sunglasses that she refused to take off and her worn-down high heels; Lacy again in the middle of the Saturday night madness; Hubert Summerlin, too, and the massive buffalo visiting me there in the middle of the night next to Hubert's smoldering campfire; the Jigglers on that lonely gray half-moon stage up at the amphitheater, juggling-juggling-juggling; Colonel James Lawrence and Gloria and Debra and little William; the busloads of blue-hairs and high school students from over in Dickinson on their way up the hill to see the show; the Old West Shooting Gallery and the bumper cars and little Lilly, watching me draw all of those silly caricatures; Willie Beck, walking to the Badlands Saloon; and me leaving New York City for North Dakota three months earlier with an empty portfolio.

Drawings are diary entries. That moment when the pen touches the page, every thought you had at that split second is somehow preserved in the drawing when you look at it again, like something a computer would somehow do, but never could. I had the drawings

now and that was something, but I never really needed them, I suppose. Memories from that particular time in life are more permanent than anything that can be said or read because they're pure and innocent in a way that memories from later in life can never be. The first time is always enduring, like riding an orange single-speed bike in the Badlands or making love, that initial recognition of a new world that before that moment never existed.

206

Epilogue

The studio is quiet this evening, quiet in a New York City sort of way—the low hum of the buses and chattering passersby down there on Broadway, the squeaking sounds of the vegetable carts rolling away for the day, the last monotonous song from the last ice-cream truck in Washington Heights.

The sun is almost gone, too, and the light here in my room—sitting here in front of my easel right now—is soft and comfortable, a familiar barroom atmosphere. I put two new paintings up on the easel a couple of hours ago—Willie Beck there in his lawn chair, laughing back at me from the great beyond in his underwear with a beer and an unlit cigarette, and then just a lawn chair.

"Heh-yup!"

I stand up and walk over to the open window. It's autumn outside, that dynamic season of passing, the leaves on quiet fire five floors down below me in the courtyard, clouds hot-pink in the dusky Atlantic twilight up above. Willie Beck's hat is hanging there on a rusty nail next to the window.

And part of my mind wanders out the window here, up past the roof of the building and on, upward, higher. And there I am, looking back down on myself, leaning out of this New York City apartment building window. The George Washington Bridge is frozen like a line drawing in the waning autumn light, and beyond that New Jersey. And beyond that further still America, rolling and tumbling for thousands of dream miles, the cities and towns out there sparkling and shining like lower constellations, and somewhere—

somewhere—out there between heaven and me, Marysville and the Badlands Saloon, and Willie Beck laughing out loud—floating—all night long.

Acknowledgments

I'd like to thank the following people for their help in bringing this book to fruition: my agent, Farley Chase, who had a hunch; my editor, Anna deVries, who had the nerve; and Carolyn and Dale Twingley, for words and pictures.

About the Author

Jonathan Twingley was born in Bismarck, North Dakota, in 1973. He took a bachelor's degree from the University of Minnesota at Moorhead in 1996 and a master of fine arts degree in illustration from the School of Visual Arts in New York City in 1998. His work has appeared in many national publications including the *Los Angeles Times*, *The New York Times*, *The New Republic*, *The Atlantic*, *The Washington Post*, *Mother Jones* and *The Wall Street Journal*. In 2003, *Print* magazine featured his work in the *New Visual Artists Review*, a showcase of twenty artists under the age of thirty. His work has also been recognized by the Society of Illustrators, *American Illustration*, *Communication Arts* magazine and the Society of Publication Designers. He lives and works in New York City.